IN THE END THE BEGINNING

Mary Steele

In the End the Beginning

Mary Steele

In the End the Beginning

Copyright © Mary Steele 2023

All rights reserved. The moral rights of the author have been asserted.

Cover artwork © 1889 books

www.1889books.co.uk
ISBN: 978-1-915045-21-8

PREFACE

This is the story of my mother's long, tormented life. Born in 1911, she was a mere 'skeleton in the family cupboard' and a stranger to her younger children until their teenage years. Local 'whisperings' and secret papers, discovered in a wooden box and buried deep inside a wardrobe, having roused my interest, I set out on a mission to discover what had happened to my absent mother who was described by neighbours and relatives as 'a lovely, intelligent woman who cared deeply for her children.' Why had she been committed to a mental asylum for almost three decades?

Over subsequent years, I gathered information from those who knew her in her younger days.

However, it was not until 1965 that I felt I could, using pen and paper, at least begin to write her story. Yet there were important gaps to be filled and appealing to Middlewood Hospital for information, I was amazed to receive a thick folder of daily recordings of her detainment there. I will be forever grateful to this kind gentleman who finally laid the ghost of my mother's past to rest and allowed me to finish writing her story based on facts included there.

It has been a long task to tell my mother's sad story and in so doing attempting to remove the stigma associated with long detainment in an asylum.

– Mary Steele 2023

Can you hear me?

Don't walk away and leave me here.
I'm still alive – I still feel fear.
The days are long, nights full of dread,
With thoughts of abandonment filling my head.

I'm trapped – can you hear me? I need to be free.
Is there nobody out there to rescue me?
I've longed for familiar footsteps, a face from days long gone.
I've been in this hell-hole for years now. I just can't carry on.

Can you hear me? I'm frightened. Does nobody care?
Am I not even a memory for someone out there?
The road I travel is lonely now. The past was all in vain.
If this is life, I never ever want to pass this way again.

CHAPTER ONE
AT THE BEGINNING – THE END

Drifting on a tranquil plain, I know the end is near. Yet there is no fear, only a feeling of great relief at finally shaking off the shackles of a long, miserable life, and the promise of eternal sleep. I turn slightly meeting the tearful gaze of a hazy young woman seated alongside, clutching my hand in hers, but a brilliant white light suddenly marring my view, I feel a strange re-awakening. An unfamiliar feeling of awareness. Maybe there is no death after all but a life beyond in which injustices in this are righted, the cards shuffled and dealt differently, and perhaps I should welcome that beckoning bright light, possibly guiding me to a better place. But wait, a familiar scene gradually emerging into view, I shudder with apprehension, try to suppress a spiritual scream of despair. This is not the vision of a new, more carefree, world! Indeed, it's a replica of the old – that I desperately wish to leave behind as death draws nearer. Oh, no – can this be that fabled prelude to death? That moment when the past flashes before your eyes? Already I am desperately afraid and recoiling at the prospect of possibly travelling again that cruel road littered with the debris of my life because this sudden clarity of thought is terrifying, as the opening pages of memory's book slowly begin to turn. My worst fears realised, that blinding light draws me, helpless and resisting, back into that painful yesteryear. Rubbing my eyes in disbelief I try to shut out the sight of a large signpost looming large, its arms outstretched in many directions, huge letters of black screaming through the greyness – SHEFFIELD – place of my birth!

As if through gradually opening curtains giving way to a theatre stage, the distant blackened sprawl of a power station slowly appears, its belching chimneys laying a dark veil over a huddled hamlet lower down the hillside overlooking Neepsend's dark industrial valley. Parkwood Springs! What memories it evokes of days long gone! Their squat chimneys emitting lazy spirals of smoke into the misty night air; tiny red-brick houses cling together along narrow cobbled streets marching downwards towards Wallace Road, an occasional tiny corner shop and public house providing necessities and temporary respite from days filled with toil and tedium. Providing solace to the masses, a sombre-looking grey, stone Methodist church appears out of place in the ungodly environment. I try to turn back but the road behind me is closed now and, peering down a narrow opening at the end of Wallace Road, I trace shadowy, descending flights of crude wooden steps giving way to a rickety bridge spanning railway lines before winding further into increasing blackness of Neepsend in the valley bottom. Multiple factories straggle its industrial floor, march along the banks of the River Don as far as the eye can see, familiar household names screaming from blackened frontages: Osborn Mushet, Neepsend Steel and Tool, Woodhead Toledo, Thomas Turton, Daniel Doncaster ,Jonas Woodhead etc. Escaping from tall chimneys, stinking plumes of black hang as a pall over the area, as night closes in rendering almost invisible rows of squat terraces and an occasional corner shop huddled beneath their shadows. Battling for supremacy, hazy street lights, a trundling tram, faint beams of light seeping from windows of public houses, scattered amongst them, barely cut through the dense industrial smog. Ghostly, a giant domed gasometer ominously rears its ugly head above the scene, keeping a watchful eye over the sprawl of the gasworks nestling in its shadow at the foot of the station steps.

Familiar smells drift down the years: stench of escaping gas, heavy aroma of fermenting malt, barley and hops, escaping from Stones' brewery further along the way. I search the mists, shuddering at the growing familiarity of the grim scene where it all began and the shrill, haunting shriek of a train strangely echoing across the void of years. I brace myself for the inevitable. Eerily, caught in faint streetlight, a ghostly figure from the distant past emerges into view; craggy profile caught in a shimmering beam of moonlight cutting through ever-thickening mist, he bends into the cold night air, making measured progress alongside the gas works before disappearing into a dark passageway punctuating a long row of tiny terraced properties as he rounds into Farfield Road. It's old Horace Fairweather! Footsteps tapping lightly on the cobblestones, his elf-like wife hurries in his wake.

Captured in faint light seeping from a dimly-lit front room window, two shadowy figures lean, side by side, against a donkey-stoned window ledge, arms folded, tongues wagging. Hair tucked beneath neatly folded turbans, floral pinafores over calf-length dresses: it's young Alice Green and Dora Bradley, routinely rounding off the day with an exchange of local gossip. Scurrying footsteps flitting through the night, Emily Turton's slight figure appears in view from the direction of the Farfield Inn, a jug of foaming ale clasped against her scrawny chest, and she appears cowed, hurrying past the gossiping pair, ears burning.

Reminding of transient, carefree days, Neepsend County School rises, majestic and mysterious, through the greyness from an isolated corner by the weir, high stone wall surrounding huge cast-iron gates allowing entry into two separate cobbled playgrounds. The words BOYS and GIRLS, etched large into its weathered stone either side of the schoolhouse door, segregating male from female and demonstrating the strict morality of the day. Its back laid against a bleak hillside, long, rectangular windows peer over a low stone wall into the murky waters of the Don, lazily winding round the backs of three narrow, cobbled streets along Penistone Road – Anlaby, Brompton, Crompton Street – known locally as the ABC streets, for convenience. Lying, stark, against the night sky the huge school bell hangs, lifeless, from a stone arch connecting twin spires, and it seems to call to me from my childhood. Conjured from the depths, ghostly figures of old friends run around the schoolyard; haunting childish voices ring across the years in their traditional games of hopscotch, I spy, tiggy etc. Some skip alone, in pairs or in groups, and I feel a painful swell of longing for those distant, fleeting days of innocence and freedom, spent under its watchful eye.

Its filthy waters lit by moonlight, how weary the Don looks, struggling to haul a heavy burden of industrial waste thrown from broken factory windows. Discarded oil drums, resting amongst the slurry and rubble laying along its banks, spilling final dregs over the water's edge to settle in multi-coloured swirls of metallic hues upon its surface and stubbornly riding its waves until plunging over the weir on its never-ending journey to the sea. Pointlessly, I shed tears but my journey proper has hardly begun and I know there is a reservoir to be drained before I reach the end of the road.

No concept of time in my spiritual state, I am grateful for sight of a huge, round-faced clock extended outward from the wall of a factory building further along Penistone Road. Quarter to ten. Clogged feet striking cobblestones, my eyes are drawn to a ragged procession of shadowy forms dutifully treading a path towards nearby factories to work, while others sleep. Clocking machine their master. Mingling with ghosts from the past, nobody knows I encroach on their lives in my final moments, mentally wander amongst them sad in the knowledge that they will make this tedious journey with boring repetition until illness, retirement or death claim them. Eavesdropping on conversations, I listen to their grumblings about programmed lives, squalid surroundings, poor living conditions, hardship, and it is clear aspirations are buried beneath the need to make a living. Eagerly searching their number, my heart sinks and I am forced to swallow my disappointment as the last man filters through the gates of Neepsend Steel and Tool, clatters across the cobbled yard and disappears into the Time House.

I realise that if one shift is about to begin, another must be ending – and maybe this time. Impatiently watching for movement in the dark, I absorb every sound long a part of my past. Metallic clang, clang, clang of rolling mills, whoosh and constant boom, boom, boom of steam hammers, rhythmic chug of a distant train, hollow ring of barrels rolling down the ramp at nearby Stones' Brewery. Throaty hoot of factory sirens piercing the night, I scan the shadowy factory yard, avidly scrutinising every grimy face emerging from the Time House doorway. Clothing black as the surrounding night, shoulders hunched, grubby sweat towels folded at the throat, voices ringing, workers wearily make their way towards yawning factory gates. Sadly, my father is not amongst them. My heart bleeds with disappointment, but firm footsteps soon treading the cobbles, an upright figure strides through faint light seeping from the weighbridge window. Back erect, head thrust skyward, it is unmistakeably my father – Herbert Sykes! I stare aghast at his chiselled features layered in grime. Step determined, he looks so much younger than the broken man I turned my back on all those years ago. A lingering look prompts an icy shudder of regret because, our parting bitter, I know he would not welcome my spiritual intrusion into his life. If only I could turn back the clock and start again, a wiser head on my shoulders. Strutting, purposefully, out of the factory gates, head held high, nose pointed to the heavens, my father hurries past colleagues making their way home along Neepsend Lane and, despite his slight stature dwarfed by others, a distinct haughtiness sets him apart. Instinctively, I want to slip my hand in his, but such familiarity would surely make him squirm, and discomfort would be mutual, his iron fist a barrier. Watching his brisk progress over the hump of Hillfoot Bridge, across tramlines along Penistone Road and up the slope of Wood Street, I feel a growing need to whisper 'sorry' in his ear.

Sitting high on the corner house, an old metal sign sets my senses racing as he rounds into Thirza Street because there it is: my old home. Nestled amidst a quadrangle of tiny houses set on a wedge of land halfway up a sloping hillside climbing to Infirmary Road, it beckons, freshly donkey-stoned doorstep and front windowsill a reminder of my mother's long endeavours. The thrill of reunion swells in my breast as my father's measured step guides me home and my cry of excitement reaches nobody's ears as he places his key in the lock, opens the door and steps into the back kitchen because there she is! My mother, Edith! Wearing a long, floral wrap-over pinafore over a calf-length skirt and home-knitted jumper, auburn hair swept high above her forehead and caught in a hairnet at the back, a welcoming grin greets my father as he enters the kitchen and, despite a relationship of few words, there is warmth between them. Tearfully looking around the tiny kitchen I can see that everything is exactly how I remember it from my younger days. Deep pot sink nestling in the corner by an open fireplace with roaring flames serving the oven alongside, highly polished ladder-back chairs tucked beneath a matching folding-leaf table with snow-white cotton cover pressed against the back wall, colourful home-pegged rug laid in front of the hearth. Kettle singing merrily on the blazing fire, familiar aroma of lavender furniture polish, black lead, and food cooking in the range alongside wafts across memory's page and my heart almost bleeds with the pain of nostalgia.

Casually planting a peck of a kiss on my mother's cheek in passing, my father hooks his coat and hat on a peg on the back of the cellar door and scrutinising them both I sadly realise that while the grime of manual labour can be washed from my father's smooth face at the end of his shift and his work be considered done, my mother has no end to her working day. Strands of grey visible amongst her dark brown hair, worry lines are already forming in her young face bearing witness to years of twenty-four-hour genuine commitment to domestic responsibility and childcare. Awkwardly leaning towards the open fire, she lifts the steaming kettle from its flames, emptying it into a tin bath in front of the hearth and adding a further huge saucepan of simmering water standing in wait on a gas ring alongside the sink. Refilling the saucepan with cold water she carefully pours it into the bath, regularly testing the temperature until satisfied. In that moment – I spot the huge bulge of late pregnancy around her waist and the face of my older brother peering down on me from a photograph above the fireplace – I realise it must be me she carries! I reach out to tenderly touch her, grasping only fresh air in my dreamy state. How infuriating this spiritual barrier between us and how I wish I could be that slight draught slipping through the weathered window frame, gently lifting her hair and brushing against her cheek. Still, so much muddied water has flowed under the bridge since I last saw her that maybe she too would shun my advances.

Clumsy splashes tell me my father is dipping his toe in the water before entering the bathtub and I respectfully close my eyes as he undresses, until the sound of displacing water tells me he is settling in the tub. For a few moments I watch him indignantly scrubbing away the day's stubborn grime reminding him of his lowly station in life, while my mother dutifully lays the table, every move meticulously performed out of respect for my father as the breadwinner. Knife to the right, fork to the left, pint pot within easy reach of a slightly extended arm to spare his efforts at the end of his tiring day.

A large bath towel warming on the clothes horse by the fireplace, my father reaches out, wrapping it discreetly around him as he emerges from the tub, and, stepping onto the hearthrug he coughs, splutters and hawks up a huge globule of soot-stained sputum from the depths of his lungs spitting it into the flames and sending a scattering of fine ash over the hearth. Immediately, I feel great sadness at the memory of those subsequent long, unbroken years of toil, cruelly snatching away those more youthful days.

Wincing in obvious discomfort, my mother presses the flat of her hand into the small of her back as she bends into the oven lifting out a domed meat and potato pie and scoops a large portion onto my father's plate. Pouring steaming tea into his personal pint pot, she places it within easy reach. Planting a gentle kiss on my father's face as he settles at the table, she slowly makes her way to a door in the corner of the kitchen calling out a weary 'Goodnight' and, making laboured progress up a narrow, winding stairway, her deep moans gradually fade into the distance. In the kitchen below, my father is too engrossed in the business of eating to notice, and I watch with a tinge of resentment his obvious taking for granted the care and attention lavished on him by a woman at such late stage of pregnancy. Though a sparkling white shirt casually opens at his throat and its sleeves are rolled up to the elbows, there is an air of superiority about him and he looks virtually noble, his back ram-rod straight, hair slicked down beneath a fine layer of Brylcreem either side of an immaculate centre parting. In fact, what a handsome man he was in those younger days! Despite those long years of daily grind, it's clear my father has retained a sense of self and independence. Yet, no clocking machine in my mother's place of work, she appears to have given up on herself as an individual and given herself to others. Resigned to being at her family's beck and call she has no time to simply be Edith.

Eleven hollow chimes from the clock on the mantelpiece stir my father and, a constant slave to time, he automatically pushes back the chair beneath him making his way into the unlit front room. A shaft of light from a gas lamp right outside the window sends his shadow dancing around the walls of a room compatible with only the most sedate style of living. Not a speck of dust had dared to settle on the highly polished arms of chintz covered fireside chairs standing either side of the hearth, gleaming sideboard beneath the window or... my eyes settle on a walnut piano along the back wall and I choke back tears. Bane of my younger days, it mocks for its vice-like grip on my early life and, watching my father collecting his briar pipe from the mantelpiece in readiness for his usual peaceful hour of relaxation and silent contemplation, I feel a pang of bitterness towards him at the memory of those wasted childhood days. Those endless days of enforced piano practice and entrapment behind a locked door; boredom-fostered resentment and anger at the ticking away of my childhood clock. Loud moans issuing from above, my father pauses and, swiftly replacing his pipe and tobacco, he closes the curtains against the night and hurries back into the kitchen. Raking over smouldering coals in the fire grate, a loud 'hiss' fills the room and a shower of dust settles on the hearth when he throws remaining tea from the teapot over them. Taking a swift glance around the room he peers into darkness beyond the window, closes the curtains and turns off the light, plunging the room into blackness.

How strange to see my dignified father standing beside the bed in his long johns, face creased with concern at the sight of my mother peering through the window in obvious distress. Long woollen coat over a flannelette nightdress she begins pacing the room and, hurrying to comfort her, my father places his arm around her shoulder but she impatiently shakes it free. Clearly upset by her rebuttal, my father climbs into bed, swiftly pulling the covers over his head to drown out her groans as he shuffles into a more comfortable position; almost instant rhythmical rise and fall of the bedclothes and heavy snoring suggests that even an exploding bomb might fail to wake him. Still pacing, my mother finally comes to rest hands pressed flat upon the dressing table, face contorted with pain as she rocks back and forth, occasionally rubbing the small of her back with both hands, and it's clear the time is drawing near.

Throughout the night she struggles but, faint light at last seeping through the sash window, things begin moving apace and, desperately clutching at the pit of her stomach, a piercing scream escapes from her gaping mouth. Urgently wrenching the bedclothes off my father, she frantically shakes him and he appears, momentarily confused, rubbing his eyes and searching the room before leaping out of bed, dressing urgently and swiftly exiting the room. Stumbling to the window, my mother breathes a draught of warm air onto an opaque windowpane, melting spidery works of art mysteriously etched into a thick coating of ice, formed overnight. Making circular movements with the palm of her hand, she clears a large porthole, anxiously peering into the misty street below as dawn begins to break over Neepsend. Overnight frost has transformed the street. Translucent icicles hang from every gutter and windowsill, cobbles sparkle with a million jewels and, the sound of heavy boots crunching over frosted cobbles, my mother presses her face close to the glass, but only the hunched form of the lamplighter emerges from the mist. Lanky body swathed in a long, dark coat, muffler folded at his throat, flat cap pressed close to his head, a dewdrop, precariously clinging to the end of his sharply pointed nose, momentarily glistens in the gas light as he passes beneath. Tapping a long pole against bedroom windows he makes his way around the quadrangle, waking again men to their labours. Snuffing out each street light on his return, he leaves the quadrangle bathed in the eerie half light of a slowly sinking moon.

In quick succession, faint light appears at bedroom windows, as residents awake to a new day, and, peering from her vantage point, my mother is visibly relieved at the sound of determined tread and scurrying feet echoing, in unison, across the silence. Casting anxious glances upwards towards the window above, Nellie Schofield swiftly takes the lead into the dark passageway and, face anxious, tread purposeful my father swiftly brings up the rear. Her family history, long-written within Neepsend, medical knowledge passed down generations, Nellie is a valued and trusted member of the community and, readily recognised in her bottle green gaberdine mackintosh, a matching woollen hat firmly pressed on a mass of unruly, mousey hair, her familiar tapping footsteps bring comfort to many in their hour of need. Gathering pace up the stairway, my mother visibly relaxes, her desperate cries ringing as Nellie enters the room, immediately throwing her hat and coat over a wicker chair by the window. Loudly calling for hot water she bends to her task.

No longer able to resist the drag of imminent birth, my mother obeys nature and, thrusting, bearing down, screaming in quick succession, every move brings her ever nearer the foot of the bed, but the birth is difficult and challenging. Knowing time is not on her side, Nellie skilfully twists and turns the ill-positioned baby in her attempt to safely deliver it into the world and, even in my ghostly state, I feel a stinging pain at every push and agonising scream. Yet maybe my reluctance to enter the world was intuitive. Maybe my newly-forming psyche was prematurely warning of what life had in store, but it's doubtful because my mother's attempts to expel me from that fluid cocoon would have been pointless against my desperate desire to resist birth to the point of death. For sure, there would have been no Alice Sykes! A moment's melancholy broken by a blood-curdling scream, my mother's thrusting and writhing propels the bloodied infant into Nellie's waiting hands. Exhausted, she falls back against the pillow and as Nellie lays the newly-swaddled infant in her arms, I can barely believe that, on the cusp of death, I have mysteriously witnessed my own entry into the world!

Now that the stresses and strains of the night are over and a quiet calm has descended, familiar sights and sounds of a Neepsend morning drift across my mind from years long gone now, as the heavy tread of clogged feet herald the arrival of workers emerging from dark passageways, faces scrubbed, work clothing still soiled from yesterday's toil. Gosh! Surely that is a young Tom Stevenson! A mere slip of a boy, with flat cap over-large for his head, large clogs weighing heavy on his young feet, newspaper parcel of sandwiches protruding from his shabby jacket pocket, mashing can swinging from his fingers; he appears a miniature of other, more mature, men making their way into Wood Street, coat collars turned up against the throat, heads bent into an icy wind, the rhythmical clatter of clogged feet against cobblestones track their progress through the mist.

Figments from the distant past: Fred Dalton, Harry Thurlow, Ted Johnson, Tom Bishop and Ben Laidlaw march towards me through the mists of time. An inheritance from long years of industrial toil, the elders amongst them cough, splutter and loudly hawk up thick sputum, angrily expelling it into the gutter along the way. At factory gates, the weary give way to the refreshed as works' sirens scream across Neepsend, some making their way home, others disappearing into the blackness of factory yards to again man bar mills, sheet mills, strip mills and forges, while people sleep, making steel of worldwide acclaim. Filthy it may be, in poverty its people, but I feel a swell of pride in the knowledge that Neepsend long played a part in cornering the market for the finest steel stamped with the mark 'Made in Sheffield.'

CHAPTER TWO
BITTERSWEET

In the blink of an eye, those early days are swept from sight as if no influence on my life. But look at me now: bustling around beyond the lighted window of a baker's shop, the words E. SYKES – BAKERS AND CONFECTIONERS proudly emblazoned over its red brick frontage. In long black dress, starched white, frilly apron and mop cap, how I dance to my mother's tune, hoisting sacks of flour from the back room, preparing bun tins, laying paper doyleys on glass cake stands in the window proudly displaying our wares. Look how my mother thrives in her new-found independence, her domestic skills finally put to profitable use. In calf-length white overall and floppy cap, barely a line creases her face as she presses mounds of dough into a row of bread tins, covers them with a muslin cloth and leaves them to prove, but throughout that short period of contentment, how were we to know that trouble was waiting in the wings?

Sudden movement outside the window catches my eye and from the misty murk of early evening, a familiar face peers in. My God! IT'S HARRY! Young face gaunt, body emaciated as if his short life had drawn the strength from him, his appearance is fleeting, but exaggerated shadow falling across the cobbles, I know he will be tracking my progress along Langsett Road at closing time, slipping into dark passageways on Wood Street along the way to watch, from a distance, until I disappear into the shadows of Thirza Street. Nevertheless, I know it will not be the end of him! One hand tucked into a shabby jacket pocket, the other occasionally lifting a cigarette to his lips, he will be carelessly leaning against the wall outside Fred's Dance Hall on Hillsborough corner on Saturday night, waiting for my emergence from my regular dance class, determined to one day gather the courage to make that first move. Still, months of perseverance have yet to pay off! It's a sort of cat and mouse game; he pursues and I shun his advances, but the chase merely adds excitement to a life daily dogged by constant piano practice. Nevertheless, my father's warning words deeply embedded, I know the dangers of venturing into such forbidden territory.

Earphone plaits curled over each ear, floral dress discreetly covering my knees, I sit, bolt upright, at the walnut piano, licking flames from the open fire dancing in its brilliant sheen, sullen face reflecting unhappiness at my captive state. Eyes firmly fixed on the music sheet propped against the music stand, fingers deftly running across the keyboard, I pay silent homage to classical works by Chopin, Beethoven, Brahms and other equally eminent composers, with an expertise born of constant repetition. However, there is anger behind every note at the dwindling of my fleeting youth, resentment at loss of freedom, and, though that spread newspaper might give the impression my father is too engrossed in reading to notice, it's a pose meant purely to deceive! As a fox waiting to pounce on its prey, he sits in that fireside chair by the hearth, ears pricked, with not a little selfishness because he basks in the glory of my skill for readily mastering complicated pieces, drawing kudos from his boasting about my prowess amongst work colleagues he daily seeks to impress. Nevertheless, unknown to him, it's common knowledge that those same colleagues merely laugh at his working-class snobbery, sniggering behind his back and hoping, one day, to witness his downfall. Maybe it seems I am at ease expertly fingering those familiar ebony and ivory keys but... is that a wrong note? Woefully shaking his head, my father calmly lays the newspaper on the table, strides purposefully across the room in my direction and I cower as he approaches his whole demeanour sending out an unmistakeable message of disapproval. Placing a firm hand on my shoulder there is no need for words as he slowly turns back the page of the song sheet, issuing a silent warning that anything less than a perfect repetition will have serious repercussions. Stiff, upright body in close proximity, booming voice ringing in my ear, his hot breath wafts across my cheek and, composure crumbling, concentration wavering, I stiffen and immediately hit the wrong note. My father's grip tightens and, immediately removing me from the piano stool, he slams down the lid, a stiff extended forefinger pointing in the direction of the doorway. A picture of misery, I make my way to the attic bedroom, the sound of my mother remonstrating with my father in the kitchen below, heartening, but I know my father will have the last word.

How bittersweet those varied flavours of home! A sanctuary from my father's constant supervision, there are both benefits and drawbacks to that cramped bedroom at the top of the house, its sloping skylight letting in light and not a little rain, old rusting bucket standing in the corner in the event of a downpour.

While summer sunshine struggles to pierce the day's gloom, various constellations valiantly battle heavy night mists for recognition, hindering my growing knowledge of celestial bodies. Winter storms were magical! Scudding clouds of black, brilliant flashes of lightning, torrents of silvery rain, wonderful sight of falling snow, all painted on that nocturnal canvas. In a medley of multi-coloured cotes further along the hillside, homing pigeons suffer the same caged existence, but how I envied their occasional flight into the wide blue yonder! A multitude of flapping wings leaving behind the filthy air of Neepsend for balmier climes, returning to circle the Don until responding to a familiar call from a lone figure patiently awaiting their return from the nearby hillside. Myself? I simply retire into solitude with a good book, but I know that, regularly chastising my father for his over-zealousness, my mother was right because a caged animal does indeed grow restless and desperate to spread its wings.

In front of my eyes, seasons come and go as if of no consequence but where were the visible signs of spring and summer in Neepsend anyway? Perhaps they simply passed me by, but how can spring warn of its coming with no crocus to lead the way, plants pushing their heads through the earth at winter's close, copulating rams and ewes signalling its imminence, or lambs telling of its arrival? No green fields in which they might gambol. What purpose do April rains serve anyway except to disturb the slurry at the bottom of the Don, further muddying its waters? What use a blazing sun when its light barely penetrates the murk and fails to brighten the ugly, man-made environment, except to somewhat warm the air and remind the world that nature still ruled? With good reason, many of its creatures have long abandoned Neepsend and yet more hardy wildlife have adapted and, scavenging food thrown from factory windows, rats inhabit the riverbank. Resident vermin controllers, feral cats, seek scraps on filthy factory floors, pigeons build homes for their young in dark crevices below blackened eves warmed by the heat of raging furnaces and human activity on the floor below. In sharp contrast, autumn is clearly audible when, in full swing, wild, gusty winds whistle and swirl around the twin spires of Hillfoot School, domed gas tanks and multiple towering chimneys; clearly visible in the dashing of waves against rocks and debris blocking the path of the Don, in scurrying people coats buttoned high against the throat, coat tails flying, gloved hands clutching flapping head scarves, flat caps and the occasional trilby. Blown off course, ducks sometimes glide to rest on its filthy water, exciting those grown used to its barren environment. Maybe, however, I was too engrossed to notice nature's changes, deceiving my parents by striking up a friendship of which my parents would never approve.

With no crystal ball in which to see the pitfalls along the way, I venture down an uncharted road, my father sitting on my shoulder, warning bells ringing in my ear. Harry waiting for me at the Farfield Inn, but a fine thread slowly binding us; nothing can hold me back and, look at me now: a new spark in my life! Long black coat billowing in the wind, gloved hand securing a cloche hat close to my head, another clutching a muslin-covered basin close to my chest, I hurry through mists casting a dark veil over Hillfoot Bridge towards the Farfield Inn face flushed with excitement. Tall and angular, the inn occupies a corner spot at the foot of Farfield Road, its two upper tiers of sash windows peering into the waters of the Don lower tier, with the words GILMOUR'S ALES etched large into its frosted glass, struggling to see beyond its wall. Hanging from a rusting chain high on the corner of the building, a colourful sign fools the less knowledgeable with its confusing declaration that it is a FREE HOUSE! Harry's gaunt face, peering over a half-frosted pane, my feet barely touch the ground over the final steps when he emerges from swing doors releasing sounds of merriment into the night. A wiry five-foot-six youth in shabby jacket and trousers, unruly sprigs of black curly hair spring from beneath the neb of a flat cap; a lit cigarette protrudes from his lips and the familiar combination of beer and tobacco drifts from his person as he approaches, a wonky grin spreading across his sharp features. Hurrying, hand in hand, through misty darkness, we part company on approaching the gates of Neepsend Steel and Tool, Harry darting out of sight behind a nearby factory wall, myself slipping into the shadows of a darkened yard, a dutiful daughter delivering a warm evening meal to a perpendicular figure standing in faint light seeping from the weighbridge window. Carried on the wind, stern words of warning weigh heavy on my return as Harry furtively emerges from his hideaway, flicking a cigarette stub into the eddying wind. Hurrying around twisting back streets, we slip into shadows alongside the high stone wall of the gas works towards the foot of the station steps in pursuit of privacy and solitude in the tiny hamlet of Parkwood Springs way above, but, what an adventure this cloak and dagger operation; a necessity: our furtive flitting around streets where walls have ears, windows eyes.

Faced with the mountainous climb up crudely-hewn planks of wood, yawning gaps between each beckoning the frail and slight to the ground way below, childhood fears surface and I cling close to Harry. Shrill whistle of an approaching train cutting across the wind, we come to rest on a bridge spanning railway lines, leaning over cast iron railings, as it passes beneath, and waving at shadowy figures of complete strangers peering from dimly-lit carriage windows until it snakes into distant darkness. Blustery winds aiding us from behind we negotiate the final flight, breathlessly arriving on the cobbles of Wallace Road. Beyond a high brick wall topped by warped cast-iron railings, a continuous row of squat houses run almost its length, blackened passageways beneath offering privacy from prying eyes possibly peering from squat houses at street level opposite. Huddled close in its shelter, Harry and I exchange life experience and, our lifestyles poles apart, I am saddened by Harry's troubled years. Born on Limbrick Road, Hillsborough, and orphaned at an early age, he had long carried the heavy burden of caring for younger siblings, only charitable donations from a spinster aunt eking out a pittance of dole money and saving them from destitution. The flame of anger still burning, he tells of his younger sister's struggle to breathe and early demise. Constant struggle, poverty and unemployment dogging his days, his life experience had been painful, turning him into a political animal with fire in his belly, venom in his voice, disillusionment in his eyes at a world in which he had little personal control. Siblings grown now, scars of the past are still visible and, outlook on life bleak, he regularly drowns his sorrows in the Farfield Inn, venting his anger in heated discussions with others facing unemployment, experiencing the same loss of purpose, pride and independence. I try to dispel his fears and encourage optimism but we both know a recession is squeezing the life out of Neepsend. Order books falling, factories failing, he is far from alone in his despair: others like him regularly seeking solace in the rowdy atmosphere of public houses ringing with the sound of jangling pianos and raucous voices. Temporary sanctuaries from a cruel world; beer frees the spirit turning pessimism to optimism, despair to euphoria, so that by the end of the evening the air is filled with a cacophony of carefree voices raised in song.

Screaming through the night, the piercing shriek of a distant train issues a stark warning, and, frantically splashing through puddles swiftly forming in gaps between cobblestones, I flee without warning, gloved hand securing my cloche hat to my head, Harry's dashing footsteps echoing in hot pursuit. Only the dim glow of a solitary street lamp and occasional faint light escaping from a front room window lights our way past the ghostly shape of the Methodist church, and, disappearing, singly, into dark shadows thrown from wagons in the railway yard, we finally emerge holding hands. Our dashing footsteps, cutting across the howling wind, prompt customers to curiously peer over stunted ships on a wavy sea etched into the half-frosted chip shop window, but a thick film of condensation mars their view. Issuing from closed doors of Hallamshire Rolling Mills, as we race by, the muffled clatter and clang of industry, raised masculine voices are possibly its swansong. Breathlessly drawing to a halt on Neepsend Lane, we lean over the Don wall and, each with an outstretched arm wrapped around the other's shoulder, silently watch the water's foaming swell in our last moments together.

All around, the night is filled with sound! Swishing and swirling of the Don, drone of a tram and the constant drumming of heavy industry drown out conversation, but, lost in a world of our own, we find peace in personal contentment. Intuitively sensing a presence, I swiftly search the night and, caught in a faint shimmer of gas light at the end of Thirza Street, a diminutive form does the same. Arm raised, eyes shaded by a spread palm, my mother stands transfixed, staring in our direction, but, suddenly animated, arms and legs moving with military precision, she indignantly struts in the direction of home. Head hung low over the Don wall I instantly empty the contents of my stomach, legs trembling when I race in hot pursuit over tramlines set in Penistone Road, Harry the last thing on my mind in my desperate bid to save my own skin. Nevertheless, a distant voice carried on the howling wind assures me he has given up the chase, swift backward glance that there is no need for guilt because he is already answering the call of muted laughter and merriment issuing from the walls of the Farfield Inn.

My father is clearly consumed with rage when I breathlessly burst into the kitchen, but my ordeal short, sharp and decidedly scary, his furious dismissal tells me it will not be the end of things. Mood sombre, I climb the stairs to the attic bedroom at the top of the house and, slipping into bed, silently mull over events of the evening, contemplating the nature of further punishment warranting an overnight delay. Shaking the fragile frame of the skylight, blustery winds make more menacing the seemingly endless night, and when morning comes on slippered feet, heavy grey mists outside the window reflect dark fears. Arms clamped either side of his waist, head thrust skyward, my father peers down the length of his nose, as if a sergeant major about to remonstrate with a raw recruit. In sober dark suit and matching waistcoat, sparkling white shirt with sharply contrasting black tie folded into an immaculate knot just below a protruding Adam's Apple, firelight plays in spit and polished toe caps and his very presence intimidates. Even his dark shadow falling, elongated and perpendicular against the back wall appears menacing. Every muscle visibly stiffening, he stands with his back to the blazing fire, curled forefinger beckoning me forward.

Nerves jangling, I cower at his feet! Dark bulges beneath glaring pink eyes tell me my behaviour has led to a sleepless night and, trembling, as an aspen leaf in the wind, I meet his steely gaze. Wisdom immediately taking precedence I adopt a hangdog expression, but morality his guiding principle, it's clear my father already considers me a wanton hussy determined to drag his name through the mud with my interest in the opposite sex. In a state of deep concentration, he makes determined progress back and forth across my path, hands firmly clasped behind his back, head bent, old floorboards objecting. Coming to an abrupt halt in front of me he hooks a stiff forefinger under my chin, sharply wrenching my head upward until we are face to face and his squinting eyes meet mine. Blushing at the unaccustomed paternal intimacy, I swiftly avert my gaze but, angrily jerking my head back in his direction, he holds it there and, a fine white foam seeping from the corners of his mouth, it is clear last night's episode is all too much for my strait-laced father. A dark silence weighing heavy, we search each other's eyes, he looking for truth, me silently pleading for leniency. Suddenly posing a threat he closes in, his stiff fingers menacingly drum along a thick leather belt hugging his waistline until finally coming to rest on a large metal buckle sitting right over his navel. Dark mood deepening, a worrying frown creases his forehead, jagged purple vein at his temple visibly pulsates and it appears the terrifying weapon is finally to be put to use, but his whole demeanour changes and at a loss he sinks into contemplative mood.

Urgently seeking support from a familiar source, he clumsily thrusts a trembling hand into his waistcoat pocket, drawing out a treasured family timepiece attached to the end of a gold chain strung across his chest. Laying it in the palm of his hand he strokes it fondly. With a reverence usually afforded things religious, he peruses its clear dial and, a strange expression creeping over his face, he falls calm. A tie to the past proving a clearly defined bloodline, it has long been part and parcel of his arrogant nature, making him look down on others with chequered histories and no such definitive connections. Passed down generations it has comforted many in times of strife and, as if caressing some beloved long-lost relative, he lovingly runs his forefinger around gleaming gold numbers in his search for inspiration. This dip into the past always works and, following a further moment of contemplation, he emerges from the experience, a different man. A strange smile lighting his face he appears to be weighing up the wisdom of ages delivered from the grave and, sensing victory, he peers down the length of his nose. Silent musings, a part of his psychological warfare, I stand mesmerised as a rabbit caught in a glaring beam of light. Pensively tucking the heirloom back into his waistcoat pocket, he makes slow descent onto a dining chair alongside the table, resting his elbow on the damask cover and propping his chin in a cupped palm. Gazing into space, he drums the fingers of his free hand against a raised kneecap, a wry expression and air of calm making it difficult to judge his mood and only the absence of a powdered wig and black gown reminds me I am not in a court of law.

In the uncomfortable silence, he rises to his full height and, face solemn, slowly unbuckles the belt at his waist ominously swinging it back and forth as he approaches. Legs astride, arms akimbo, his sallow cheeks infuse with blood, the end of his nose assumes a rich shade of crimson as he leans forward, cracking the whip close to my quivering legs. Instantly, I freeze, but, arrogant stance again collapsing, he lets the whip slip from his hand, his eyes glaze over, shoulders droop and, every drop of colour draining from his face, he appears to be suffering something akin to a seizure. As if worrying thoughts steal his confidence, he places a conciliatory hand on mine, but years of hard discipline forging an unbridgeable divide, discomfort is mutual and, instantly aware his momentary lapse might undermine his authority, he quickly pulls it away. Composure swiftly recovered, his every sinew stiffens and, again perpendicular, he recovers the belt, flicking it sharply so that a rush of air lifts the hem of my skirt as it lashes the back of my legs. An agonised scream escaping, I hold back my tears because what I suspect my father might mistake for remorse was merely a display of self-pity prompted by a vision of Harry's despondent face peering from the window of the Farfield Inn.

It is indeed a despondent Harry, nightly peering into the dark, misty night from the window of the Farfield Inn, vainly searching the Neepsend mists, disappointed at the sight of my mother's rounded form regularly hurrying over Hillfoot Bridge, a familiar muslin-covered basin tucked close to her chest. Nevertheless, a surfeit of Gilmour's Ales his driving force, he begins a ritual trek in the full knowledge that my father is baying for his blood. Determined to get to the bottom of things, he daily climbs the slope of Wood Street and, a shadowy figure casually leaning against a lamp post at the end of Thirza Street, he keeps a silent vigil, cigarette smoke constantly drifting across its faint light. A vain errand, he later retraces his steps, a miserable expression on his face.

CHAPTER THREE
A PRICE TO PAY

Snowy blizzards transform the area. Swirling around towering chimneys, twin spires of Hillfoot County School and giant, domed gasometers, it lays a blanket of white over cobbled streets and carpets the debris-strewn banks of the Don. Tram wires strain under its weight, squat houses assume the appearance of quaint cottages, and, a picture postcard scene, Neepsend huddles under its winter coat, but days of heavy fall render dangerous its many climbing slopes. The weather at its worst now, only a lone figure braves the elements, coat collar turned to meet the back of his flat cap, one lapel tucked inside the other to keep warm his throat. Warily negotiating the slippery upward slope of Wood Street, Harry leans into the driving snowstorm, cheeks mottled, red nose shining as a beacon, startled expression caught in shimmering light thrown from a nearby street lamp as he stops dead on the turn of Thirza Street at the sight of my shadowy form struggling homeward. His shrill whistle prompts a knee-jerk reaction and, abandoning all caution, I slither along the icy surface; buttoned boots leave the ground, gloved hands clutch at fresh air, and, taking flight, I quickly come to rest in the thick snow, cloche hat at a distance. Concerned face looming through the flurries, Harry swiftly hauls me to my feet and, desperately searching the street for possible prying onlookers, I attempt a clumsy escape but, firmly gripping my coat sleeve, he holds me there awhile. Retrieving my hat from the snow, he holds it out of reach, mockingly twirling it on the end of a forefinger.

Crunching footsteps heralding the approach of a snow-covered figure further along the street, I panic and make a frantic bid to escape, but he draws me close, placing the hat firmly back on my head and whispering in my ear as he turns to go. Mood buoyant, he dips into the snowstorm and the night swallows him.

Even the gaudy red light outside the Queens public house appears to warn of danger and, designed to deter rather than welcome me in; hesitant, I tug at Harry's sleeve, reluctant to cross the threshold of a place my father considers to be a den of iniquity filled with patrons he considers to be the wastrels of society. Just one step will break my father's hold and demonstrate my loyalty to Harry but it's as if a huge metal barrier holds me back, making me seriously reconsider the wisdom of my defiant move. Nevertheless, finally succumbing to Harry's powers of persuasion, I place a damp palm in his as he gently encourages me through the heavy swing doors.

It's difficult to see through dim lighting and a haze of cigarette smoke forming a grey canopy over the scene, but, at first glance, it all appears innocent enough. Caught in the glow of a roaring fire a kindred musician sits at an old piano, thumbing through tattered pages of an old song sheet propped on a music stand. Shadowy, animated figures huddle around rectangular and circular tables and only a rich tapestry of people sharing friendly camaraderie confronts me, but, no doubt my father would violently disapprove of the occasional raunchy innuendo greeted by loud guffawing in this mainly male environment. Immune to the buzz of animated conversations, some are deeply engrossed, poring over spread hand of cards or dominoes, heads bent, flimsy self-made cigarettes, loosely hanging from pursed lips, sending wisps of smoke into the heavily-burdened atmosphere. Occasionally blindly reaching for pint pots from the table, some gulp at foaming ale, returning the glass with a precision born of long experience, neither spilling a drop nor disturbing their train of thought.

A mere hive of social activity, it seems employment and a cushioned existence has blinded my father, but lights going out at many factories around Neepsend, his intolerant views might dissolve with his own employment. A smattering of women in turbans, cloche or feathered hats defy society's unwritten rule, braving the male-orientated domain and risking being labelled harlots, hussies etc. Steering me amongst the chattering throng, Harry leads me to a door in the far corner of the room close by the bar. At that moment, a tinkling of introductory notes heralds a momentary deathly hush of anticipation and a rousing miscellany of hoarse, coarse and occasionally melodious voices rock the room with a lively rendition of 'My Old Man Says Follow the Van,' quickly reaching a lively crescendo. A sharp contrast to my own sedate musical presentations under the fastidious gaze of my impatient father, the infectious sound brings primeval instincts to the fore and I hum softly to the tune as Harry leads me into the privacy of the back room.

Captivated by the lively atmosphere and the prospect of being alone with Harry, I am already willing the night to stretch forever. Gas mantles and flickering flames in the fire grate dimly light the back room, dancing shadows beckon me into an atmosphere laden with must and lingering tobacco, and, hanging from a picture rail close to the ceiling, faded photographs tell of a bygone age. Cold draughts seep through ill-fitting window frames, prompting thoughts of customers long gone from the world returning for another taste of halcyon days once spent there. By the time Harry returns bearing a pint of ale and a glass of orange on a tin tray, vivid imagination has worked overtime and I snuggle close. Raised voices, laughter, bawdy music, stomping of feet drifting through old walls transport me into another, more carefree world and, wrapped in the warmth of seclusion, we laugh and chat with natural ease. When rousing applause and clanging bell all too soon bring the evening to a close, my departure is tinged with sadness but, strolling round misty back streets, arms linked, Harry and I are both exhilarated and, when he plants a kiss on my cheek at the end of Thirza Street, I am intoxicated purely by the thrill of it all.

Memories of that magical night sustain me throughout a week of long, boring hours of piano practice and, uplifted, I apply myself with renewed effort. In the fireside chair my father relaxes, spread newspaper laid across his knees, face spread in a contented grin, feet tapping to a near perfect rendition of Handel's Largo. Indeed, his chest swelling with pride, I swear I can hear him softly humming in tune with the music.

Saturday nights take on a different meaning. A regular part of the throng in the Queens, we no longer retire to the solitude of the back room, instead calling out a friendly greeting to all and sundry on entering. Settling amongst them, Harry and I join in the revelry and, a part of the jostling throng, new friendships compensate for solitary hours at the piano throughout seemingly endless weekdays, but still my father is never far from my mind. If he could see me sitting in the midst of jostling women, carelessly hoisting their skirts in an unseemly can-can, hear my carefree laughter at the sight of an animated figure performing a skilful accompaniment to the jangling piano with a pair of tablespoons cupped together like castanets, my enthusiastic clapping as he rhythmically raps them against a raised knee or flexed elbow, he would be foaming at the mouth.

At the closing bell, the grand finale would see him almost expire. Final dregs drained from every glass, 'Time' called and lights dimmed, revellers take swift advantage of closing moments. Inhibitions released, some men carelessly throw their arms around female companions, kissing them drunkenly to the sound of 'Goodnight Sweetheart', deafening applause, shrill whistles and raucous calls for more. Others perform rhythmical clog dances along the aisles, singing drunkenly to the strains of 'Show Me the Way to Go Home' and sending it echoing across the night as they depart to make their unsteady way home. If my father was to witness my mingling with the highly intoxicated on departing, I know he would haul me home with a firm hand gripping my shoulder for heaping shame on his pristine character, but the exciting atmosphere beckons despite its dangers. However, there is a price to pay for this deception. On Sunday nights, seated on fireside chairs either side of a blazing fire, my parents drift onto a peaceful plane to the perfect strains of various classical pieces. Heads resting against neatly embroidered chair back covers, eyes closed, feet resting on the fender, minds at peace in the knowledge that my future has at last been secured. In fact, unknown to either, my future is suddenly very much in doubt.

Mood sombre, eyes bulbous, nose red from much crying, I drag my feet over the cobbles of Hillfoot Bridge towards a lone figure standing in the shadows of a towering, domed gas tank at the head of Farfield Road. Shrugging off attempts to chivvy me into a more cheerful mood, I reject Harry's proffered hand and walk, shrouded in misery, a few paces behind around Neepsend's roaming back streets, regularly pressing a damp handkerchief against my eyes. Intuitive females in the Queens immediately identify my problem, as Harry steers me amongst them to the privacy of the back room and, tipping a supportive wink, discreetly dispensing with friendly banter, they smile knowingly as I pass because some have once walked under the same shadow.

Despite a roaring fire warming the back room, a distinct chill, not attributable to haunting spirits, hangs in the air and, whichever way I mentally prepare to present the news while Harry is at the bar, I can find no simple way to cushion him from the blow. Wary of my strange mood on his return he eyes me thoughtfully as he settles alongside me at a rounded table close by the hearth, flickering flames from a fire smouldering in the grate sending his dark shadow flitting around dimly lit walls.

Without warning the grim news is out in the open shocking us both and, spluttering, Harry sends a fine spray of beer into the air, firelight plays along his waxen cheeks, his Adam's apple frantically bobs up and down, eyes bulge and, swiftly draining his glass he rushes to the bar for a refill. Sinking my head into cupped hands I weep with despair at his floundering, and urgent, repeated visits to the bar in his desperate need for liquid sustenance. In my sobriety, concentrating only on my own terrible predicament, I mentally search every avenue for means of escape, but, the hollow ring of a huge bell on the end of the bar signalling closing time, defeat inevitably stares me in the face. The night lost in silent contemplation, I link my arm in Harry's, helping him drunkenly negotiate a path between the many tables. Friends tactfully avert their gaze as I aid him, stumbling, along Infirmary Road. Forced to abandon him halfway along the homeward journey, leaden feet hinder my progress along the final stretch, and it's a quizzical pair watching me immediately disappear up the stairway in order to avoid an inquisition on red swollen eyes and crimson nose.

Troubled expression and pallid complexion attracting parental concern, I struggle to ward off searching questions, and blind panic makes me see Harry in a different light. No longer tripping carefree, over Hillfoot Bridge towards a shadowy form caught in the faint glow of a gas lamp by the gas works, my heart is heavy and burdened with the worry of it all. No welcoming smile or light in his eye on my approach, Harry also looks burdened and unhappy, and it's clear a distance has been forged. An insurmountable problem dividing us, it's a sombre reunion. Only the haunting shriek of an approaching train breaks the miserable silence, and intuitively I know natural instincts will be urging him to his usual escape route in a bid to drown his sorrows, but the solution to this problem won't be found at the bottom of a glass. No such means of escape for myself, only my mother's keen eyes peering, strangely, in my direction as if already suspicious. Terrified of rejection and its unthinkable consequences, I desperately throw my head against his chest, body heaving with desperate sobs, but, mutual feelings flooding back, we cling together, drawing strength from each other. Nevertheless, we both know an uncertain future is beckoning.

Flickering flames of a paraffin lamp searching the darkness of the backyard, purposeful tread warns of my father's imminent return from the outside toilet and, gradually emerging from the shadows, he draws to a halt outside the kitchen window. Snuffing out the paraffin lamp, he returns it to a hook alongside the back door and, habitually peering in, his face changes and his body visibly sways at the sight of Harry and I standing there, our backs to the kitchen range, arms entwined in mutual support.

If either of us thought we could imagine the depths of his fury, we were both seriously mistaken because the door rocks on its hinges as he thrusts it swiftly open. Baring his teeth in his breathless haste, he leaps over the threshold, contorted face closing in. Nostrils flaring, a stiff forefinger jabs at the tip of Harry's nose and, his grip on my arm quickly relaxing, I fear he is going to flee but my father holds him fast in his hateful gaze. Facial muscles twitching, body shaking with rage he looks set to physically attack and, every ounce of mental and physical strength ebbing, I sidle closer to Harry clutching his hand to support my weakening frame and thwarting his own obvious intention to run.

Interpreting the innocent, spontaneous move as a deliberate gesture of defiance my father rocks on the spot and out of control he glares vacantly into space, eyes bulging. Unable to bear the strain any longer, the dreaded words again slip from my lips and in the stunned silence my father is suddenly as a man possessed. Stomping in his blind fury, he appears to be doing a war dance. Fists and teeth clenched, he lunges at Harry but I urgently leap between them and, rearing backward, my father's life appears immediately at risk when he lands, with a deafening thud, on a dining chair by the table. Face drained, arms hanging loosely by his side, he helplessly rocks with the chair until it settles back on all fours. Gaping eyes stare blankly into space.

Time stands still. He draws the trusted family heirloom from his waistcoat pocket, laying it is the palm of his hand. Bloodshot eyes frantically search for answers and in the oppressive silence, unseen ancestors suddenly bring about a miraculous transformation. A pale pink hue creeping over sunken cheekbones, he begins to recover, instinctively performing a ritual, symbolic of having received satisfactory assistance. Vigorously rubbing the watch face against the front of his trousers he carries out a final inspection of its gleaming face and, carefully replacing it in his waistcoat pocket, he loudly clears his throat six times precisely. Fiddling with the immaculate knot at his throat, he pointlessly teases it from side to side returning it to the self-same spot and, rising slowly, begins pacing across my path, carrying with him the ominous air of a man sensing certain victory. Drawing to an abrupt halt right in front of us, he thrusts his face forward, eyes narrowing, every furrowed line deepening as he examines us both at close range. Momentarily slipping into a trance-like state, he appears to be giving final consideration to his plan and it's hard to resist the temptation to beg forgiveness because I don't need reminding that my behaviour has brought shame upon the whole family, that attempts to rear me in the correct manner have come to nothing and every innocent member will be subjected to innuendo and whispered gossip in this cramped community.

Emerging from his ponderings, my father's beady eyes flit, furiously, over us both and, myself on the verge of collapse, I feel Harry's body stiffen, see movement at his feet and fear he may be about to make a break for the door. My father appears to fear the same but, confidence boosted by advice delivered by those long resting beyond the grave, he stands tall and blocks his path. Standing, four-square in front of us, a thumb tucked into each armpit, splayed fingers of each hand resting upon his swiftly rising and falling chest, his hateful eyes examine my waistline. Face a pale shade of grey, he appears nauseous at the mere thought of an offspring of Harry's nestling there and, glaring down the line of his nose, he loses control. Grabbing a lapel of Harry's jacket in each clenched fist he draws him close until their noses almost touch and, fingers blanching, he shakes him violently, chest heaving, pure hatred writ large upon his face. In the heat of the moment, common sense becomes a casualty and, leaving two startled people in my wake, I flee for the stair's door. Breathlessly dashing up the narrow stairway to the attic bedroom, tears stream down my face, on carelessly thrusting my belongings into a suitcase, and, in those final, heart-wrenching, moments, I take a long lingering look around the tiny attic bedroom long my refuge from the storms of life, carefully tucking everything into my memory box to carry with me into the unknown future.

Falling, limp, against the back wall, my father is clearly numb with shock when I burst back into the kitchen, bulging suitcase swinging from my fingers and, taking swift advantage, Harry swiftly wrests it from my hand, clumsily lifts the sneck on the back door and hauls me into the safety of the back yard. Shocked by the speed of it all I momentarily pause and gasp for air, but, a desperate cry issuing from the direction of the back door, I sneak a final backward glance. Mouth gaping my father slumps, awkwardly, against the door jamb and I feel a loss akin to bereavement, but the deafening crash of a hastily slammed door, startling, I urgently grasp Harry's hand and scuttle with him along the passageway in full knowledge of the fact that there will be no turning back.

Black silhouettes laid against a darkening skyline, the old school, domed gas tanks, angular factories, rear through thickening mist of closing day and, the loud, metallic ring and monotonous thud of industrious activity echoing across the stillness, Neepsend appears sinister and unfriendly in our helplessness. Faint lights fading from front room windows, curtains closing in the Farfield Inn, even the Don appears to be sleeping, its waters still and host to a full moon, but while others retire for the night, we are in limbo and destined to walk the cold, empty streets in a bid to find a bed for the night.

Neepsend's cobbled streets twist, turn and climb but, though terraced blocks of squat houses roam over their length, empty properties are like gold dust. The unemployed, threatened with loss of government allowances and eviction for sub-letting their rented homes, people are wary and, early bravado lost in reality, door after door closing in our faces, we finally come to terms with the seriousness of our situation. Dark clouds gathering, icy raindrops splatter the cobblestones, a chill wind blows scraps of paper across our path and, panic setting in, we are at loggerheads.

Washing the streets, a sudden deluge sends us hurtling for cover beneath a dark passageway breaking a terraced row of old properties on the brow of Whitehouse Lane. In front of a dimly lit window, Harry draws me to a sudden halt. Thrusting his head close to the glass, a huge grin lights his face as he hauls me alongside directing my attention to a neat square of paper propped in front of a pristine lace curtain. With the aid of faint light escaping through a chink in the curtains, he reads aloud bold copperplate writing advertising ROOM TO LET. At that very moment, blocked guttering overhead sends a torrent of freezing cold water over us, both its loud whoosh and noisy splattering across the cobblestones prompting a wizened face to peer, warily, around the edge of the curtain. Hastily opening the door, the elderly lady clamps a scrawny hand across her mouth mortified at the sight of us standing there, arms hung limply by our sides, headgear drenched. Mouth gaping, she swiftly retreats from the doorway frantically beckoning us over a freshly donkey-stoned doorstep into an immaculate front room lit only by a blazing fire.

Dripping water onto a welcome mat, we absorb the warm, cosy atmosphere. Drifting from a domed Bakelite wireless, gentle strains of the Barcarole instantly revive memories of home and I choke back tears as the stranger scurries across the room, coming to a halt with her back towards the blazing fire. Lifting round, wire-rimmed spectacles from the bridge of a short, pointed nose, she draws a snow-white, lace-trimmed handkerchief from her sleeve, briskly clearing a film of condensation from each lens before replacing them. Scrutinising us both through squinted eyes, she strangely peers over their rim. A gnarled, quivering hand reaching for Harry's, another pressing gently on my forearm, she apologises profusely and I swear there are tears in her eyes when Harry warmly returns the gesture, his face spread in a wide, reassuring smile. A stiff finger directing us towards fireside chairs, standing either side of the hearth, she hurries from the room, returning with a snow-white towel folded over each arm, an outstretched hand reaching for our soaked outer clothing. Draping them over a clothes horse standing in an alcove alongside the hearth, hooking Harry's flat cap and my cloche hat over each end post she hurries back into the kitchen, returning with two cups of tea and two pieces of home-baked cherry cake on a tin tray. In that moment, I couldn't help thinking that fate had played a part in delivering us into the hands of such a warm, kind lady as Ellen Thompson and as Handel's Messiah drifts from the wireless, I feel the hand of God at play.

The product of advancing years, a dowager's hump gives the impression of pushing forward Ellen's small head, with fine strands of greying hair drawn into a flimsy bun at the back. Simple, long black dress with white starched collar and cuffs gives the impression of an elderly schoolmistress, but pale blue eyes, sunken, thin lips, pale, cheeks, sallow, time has clearly taken its toll. Humility, however, belies her stern persona as she lifts a poker from a stand on the corner of the hearth, dipping it into fading orange coals in the grate and stirring them until a flare of brilliant orange flames highlights a plump mole, sprouting two forked hairs, sitting right on the edge of her chin. Turning her back to the fire she hoists the hem of her skirt upwards in both hands exposing spindly legs to the flames, and, a dark shadow playfully flitting around the back wall, mimics her every move. Pulling forward a low pouffe, she perches between us and, long legs forced towards her chin, she almost squats. Grotesque now, the dancing shadow finally comes to rest, unflatteringly exaggerating the arch of her back, extending her nose and lengthening her chin so that her profile resembles that of a witch. Nevertheless, palms pressed together against her lips in praying mode, head bent, a shaft of light sneaking through a small gap at the edge of the curtain, she presents a more angelic pose. Suddenly aware of the protrusion at her chin she fondles it between forefinger and thumb and, scrutinising us both, gradually teases our tale of woe from a shame-faced Harry.

Outside, wintry winds howl like a pack of prairie wolves, moan mournfully on being sucked into the hollow passageway alongside, and rain lashing the windowpane; I give way to my fears. Immediately, Ellen places a comforting hand in mine, squeezing it gently as a sobering National Anthem signals a respectful two minutes silence and the end of broadcasting for the day. To a background of muffled sobs, Harry and Ellen chat quietly and though embers slowly die in the grate and a damp chill settles over the room, the atmosphere is soon warmed when mutual handshakes seal a tenancy agreement and promise of future friendship.

Family history is long written within the walls of the old house; Ellen cheerfully guides us up the precariously narrow stairway, flickering candle lighting the way, groaning stair treads and flitting, misshapen shadows unsettling. Caught in a halo of candlelight, she leads us along a narrow landing into a darkened bedroom at the back of the house and, curtains wide apart, the pallid face of the moon peers in. A draught of cold air mischievously playing around the candle's flickering flame, Ellen shields it with a cupped hand on her way to a kidney-shaped dressing table. Setting down the candle she snuffs out its flame and, drawing a match from a box alongside, a burst of yellow flame lights the darkness as she applies it to a gas mantle suspended from the ceiling, leaving the room bathed in faint purple light. Shutting out the inquisitive face of the moon she draws the curtains over the window, smiling warmly as she hurries towards the door, her soft voice calling 'Goodnight' on closing it behind her.

Strewn with reminders of a previous occupant, the room is ghostly in the gaslight. As if Ellen is desperately attempting to preserve precious memories and ease the pain of loss, it appears a shrine to her recently departed, a neat pin-striped suit still hanging on a coat hanger over the wardrobe door, briar pipe sending off the lingering aroma of stale tobacco, keeping him close. Peering from an old wooden picture frame hanging high above the bed, a man of advanced years appears to watch, through piercing eyes, our every move and certain I can feel his ghostly presence, goose pimples form along the surface of my skin.

Swiftly slipping into bed, I sidle close to Harry, but wild winds performing a frenzied dance around multiple chimney pots, floorboards mysteriously contracting and expanding, the night appears fraught with danger. Torrential rain lashing the sash window, curtains billowing and sinking to rest under the force of intruding draughts, the old house almost rocks on its foundations. Sensing resentment in that piercing gaze above, I curl into a tight ball in the small of Harry's back and finally pull the covers over my head but throughout the long night, dwelling on thoughts of home, sleep evades me and by the time a wintry early morning sun sneaks through the curtains, the starched pillow beneath my head is wet through with tears of unhappiness.

CHAPTER FOUR
A SPARK OF HOPE

Our lives on Whitehouse Lane gradually slipping into a natural rhythm, Ellen finally finds peace in her twilight years, myself a substitute mother. Unemployment continues to dog Harry's days but despite cardboard signs hanging from lengths of string over factory gates stating NO VACANCIES, he daily joins others leaning against a blackened factory wall alongside, in the hope that some misdeed or misunderstanding might result in dismissal of a worker at some point during the day. Kindred spirits, huddled groups of men, stripped of dignity and hope, vent their disenchantment on street corners and, on the hump of Hillfoot Bridge, their misery clearly reflected in faces looking back on them from the Don below in moments of quiet contemplation.

Each weekend, in the Farfield Inn, Harry joins others poring over problems around a glass-strewn table, and a volatile cocktail: foaming pints of beer and political debate inflame passions of men facing daily struggle, and he is in his element smoothing fiery debate and steering things to an agreeable conclusion. His mood a fair barometer of success, I learn to live with his erratic behaviour on his return. Alienated from the family scene, outside interests consume his days, and, on Friday night, Ellen settles by the fireside in the front room, myself at the piano indulging awhile in our mutual love of classical music of Ellen's choosing.

On just such a night, Handel's Water Music heralds a stirring. In quick succession agonising pains force me forward and both hands roaming, carelessly, across the keyboard, the music ends with a jangling of discordant notes. Rudely roused from her musings, Ellen bustles across the room thrusting her anxious face into the night and, urgently calling, miraculously catches Harry's attention when he pauses on the cobbles to light a cigarette. One hand clamping his flat cap close to his head, jacket tails flying, wide trouser legs flapping round his ankles he speeds through the night, a comical shadow falling at right angles up the walls of houses, running alongside at equal speed. Programmed to events concerning new arrivals in the neighbourhood, Nellie immediately identifies the owner of dashing footsteps clattering over the cobbled yard and, silencing the crackling voice of the BBC issuing from the old wireless, she pulls a voluminous bottle-green mackintosh over her spreading frame. Pressing a matching woollen hat close to a mass of wild, greying hair, she ambles over the threshold onto the cobbled back yard, almost colliding with a breathless Harry emerging from a nearby passageway, a beckoning hand flapping wildly over his shoulder when he races back up Whitehouse Lane. Negotiating the rising slope at a snail's pace, Nellie waddles in his wake. In the distance, a shadowy form leans over the doorstep of the tiny house on the brow of the hill, one hand urgently encouraging her on, the other holding an indignant Harry at bay, but, despite anguished screams escaping into the night, Nellie labours up the final stretch and, one foot pressed against the doorstep, she gasps for air.

Over recent years, many have wondered how she survives the rigours of her calling her services called upon at all hours of night and day. Suffering the worst and savouring the best of weathers she can be seen sometimes strolling, sometimes attempting to hurry but always struggling for breath around the cramped, climbing streets of Neepsend. Struggling up the narrow stairway, Nellie hauls her ample frame into the bedroom and, plump cheeks fused with blood, it appears her next step will see her expire. A piercing scream reverberating around the four walls, she swiftly hooks her coat over the corner of the open wardrobe door and hurries to the bedside, little intervention necessary when the newly born slithers, unaided, onto a bloodied bed sheet. Frantic shrieking of the newly born echoing around the whole house brings Harry's pounding footsteps racing upward until he arrives, breathless, in the bedroom, kettle of boiling water in one hand, steaming saucepan in the other.

Life on Whitehouse Lane benefits us all. Harry regaining the freedom of his bachelor days, me content with motherhood, Ellen secure in the knowledge that the prospect of a solitary life no longer casts a dark shadow over her future. Even the old house appears to have taken on a new lease of life, lusty screams of new life ringing within its walls. Instead of mourning every speck of dust settling on polished wood, every smear on sparkling glass, Ellen wallows in family life. Worldly-wise, she proves a wonderful aid in my first weeks of motherhood her pride in the newly born clearly matching my own as she peers through a fine film of condensation at the kitchen window, watching snow-white washing blowing in the wind on the line strung across the back yard, no doubt remembering that the last time there was such a sight was when her own mother had thrust her into the world under that very roof.

Troubles of the past gradually fading from memory, another dark shadow begins creeping over the world and, local and national events deteriorating, Harry is drawn into the drama of it all. Talk of war in the air, unemployment and poverty blighting many lives, problems are rife and people growing restless. Politics formed by painful life experience, Harry is ripe for the cause and, involving himself with others of a similar persuasion, he is becoming a stranger. Courtesy of appreciative friends admiringly hanging onto his every political solution, copious amounts of beer in the Farfield regularly render him almost legless and staggering footsteps can often be heard climbing the slope of Whitehouse Lane late into the night. Throwing up sash windows, neighbours angrily bawl into the street for silence setting off a chain reaction of barking dogs. Some shake their heads in disgust at the sight of him drunkenly weaving his way home, a bawdy song ringing across the night throughout his clumsy attempts to locate the keyhole with his key before stumbling over a nearby doorstep. Three missing rent payments and several complaints from neighbours threaten to spark the first altercation, posing a dilemma for Ellen. Despite secretly praying matters will resolve themselves, they merely escalate, backing her into a corner and threatening confrontation. But things come to a head of their own accord.

Ferocious barking of an anxious dog, waking Ellen from a troubled sleep, she shuffles into a sitting position, her back resting against the headboard, ears pricked at the sound of approaching staggering footsteps. Slipping out of bed she hurries, barefoot, to the window, anxiously peering into the street below and the sound of a tremulous voice singing 'Goodbye Dolly I Must Leave You' echoes across the witching hour. With the aid of a nearby street lamp, Ellen watches Harry come to a staggering halt outside the house opposite, tuneless song fading. Clumsily wobbling he leans forward striking a match against the cobblestones, after several unsuccessful attempts, finally setting aglow the end of a flimsy, self-made cigarette, dangling from the corner of his mouth. Sniffing the air, the inquisitive dog approaches and yapping shrilly it encircles him. Veering, from side to side, Harry attempts a clumsy escape, finally admitting defeat and coming to rest with his backside precariously perched on a narrow windowsill. Tapping his thigh with an open palm he encourages the excited dog closer, scratching the nape of its neck, until, whimpering in gratitude, it settles contentedly at his feet, nose pressed against the toe of his shoe. Under Ellen's furious gaze he sits, staring vacantly into the darkness, a stupid, alcohol-fuelled, grin on his face, cigarette stubs gathering at his feet.

Flinging a final cigarette stub into the gutter, he makes unsteady progress home, canine companion trotting happily by his side, tail wagging. A crude raucous version of the National Anthem rings across the silence and, "God save our gracious cat, feed him on bread and fat der, der, der, der" disturbing and offending many, windows are clumsily thrown wide. When the tuneless warbling encourages the stray dog to lift its head high and howl to the moon and a chorus of nearby dogs join in accompaniment, furious voices bellow across the night. Consumed with rage, Ellen slams shut the window and, long flannelette nightdress flapping, scrawny hands feeling their way along the narrow, unlit stairway, she throws open the front door hauling a startled Harry indoors by the lapel of his jacket. Sensing danger, the shocked dog howls in fear and, tail tucked tightly between its legs, it scuttles off into the night. Unexpectedly released, Harry stumbles across the front room landing, arms outstretched, against the back wall. Though there is no indication that his befuddled brain has the capacity to absorb her words, Ellen fires a warning shot in his ear, conscience pricked, as she hurries from the room. Heart heavy, she treads a weary path up the narrow stairway but stair treads soon creaking under staggering feet, vibrato voice striking up an encore, disturbed child screaming, she hurries out of bed onto the landing. In quick succession the song ends abruptly, bedsprings groan under the weight of a helpless body, instant snoring filters through back bedroom walls. Hurrying to the comfort of her warm bed she slips into restless sleep, relieved intervention had been justified.

The incident passes without mention but, Harry keeps a wide berth and Ellen is wary that the atmosphere in that tiny house on Whitehouse Lane was tense and uncomfortable. Ellen wonders whether the sudden change in Harry's daily routine is a product of her earlier intervention. In fact, it is completely unrelated and stemmed from a recently hatched plan, designed to resolve pressing financial problems. In the dark of night Harry embellishes its benefits, creating a wonderful vision of a bright future, and gradually winning me over, but his rash promise to resist the lure of the Farfield as part of the bargain, leaves me with deep reservations. Nevertheless, a man on a mission, he daily struts down Whitehouse Lane, a renewed spring in his step. Nightly returns, gait unsteady, lit cigarette loosely dangling from his lips.

Subsequently plagued by nightmare visions of my father, horns protruding either side of his head as if the Devil Incarnate, I pray Harry's enthusiasm will wane with the passage of time, but, just when I think it has withered and died, he bursts through the back door whooping with delight. Excitedly gripping either side of my waist he spins me in a giddy circle, suddenly bringing me to rest in front of him, a mischievous twinkle in his eye. A crooked smile lighting his face he draws me in, comically outlining the benefits of his plan and embellishing it with hilarious detail, leaving us both in fits of laughter. Dwelling on his words in the privacy of the outside toilet, I can't help chuckling but my serious side soon reins me in, forcing me to seriously consider the move designed to set our lives on a more stable footing. Despite its obvious pitfalls, however, the idea of a measure of freedom and opportunity to meet old friends again is tempting.

CHAPTER FIVE
A HEAVY LOAD

While autumn paints some landscapes in rustic colours, nature wreaks cruel revenge for man's destruction of his habitat daubing Neepsend in dingy shades of black and grey. Many of its powers redundant, there is barely a blade of grass to lay to rest until spring, no green bushes to give up ripened fruits or trees to dress in many shades of brown, orange or gold before discharging nourishing nuts to earth. Its unnatural environment no provider, rarely a fox, badger or squirrel ventures to its door in search of seasonal fare. Instead, autumn sends back decades of filth on squally showers in the form of heavy, dank fog so that night appears to merge with day. Venting her anger on the innocent, nature shows no mercy and, winter around the corner, heavy black cloud hangs low, polluted rain drives through darkened streets in sheets, freezing fog hovers over dark factories. Neepsend little more than a dark scar on the landscape, tall chimneys a blot on the skyline, only the occasional trail of stinking smoke rides on the wind, but amongst desolation, the monotonous 'boom' of a lone steam hammer tolls the death knell of collapsing industry.

It is as if the miserable world outside has drifted through the open doors of Neepsend Steel and Tool, its atmosphere oppressive and heavily laden with filth, ceiling host to massive light bulbs encased in huge, metal shades struggling to cast light over industrious activity below. Metal-lined floors exaggerate every sound. The monotonous whirr of a flywheel spinning at speed, high-pitched shriek of turning rolls, spindles and boxes clanging with every revolution, metallic clang of heavy metal slabs hitting the floor, echoing tread of clogged feet, voices calling out collectively battering the eardrums and filtering, muffled, into the street beyond. Greasing the rolls for ease of turning, a smouldering mixture of graphite and tallow emits a trail of thick, black smoke into the already burdened atmosphere, stinging the eyes and searing the nostrils with its putrid stench. In the midst of darkness brilliant light escaping from ill-fitting doors of a roaring furnace outlines, in arcs of orange, dark silhouettes bending up and down, thrusting red-hot metal through turning rolls. Flat caps slightly tilted, grubby sweat towels folded at the throat, teeth pearly white against soot-black faces grimacing in the scorching heat.

At the top of a nearby flight of metal steps, my father sits upright at his office desk, sifting through papers in his 'IN' tray. No longer the organised but the organiser, a calf-length brown dustcoat signifies his elevated position in the workforce. Promotion further inflating his ego he struts to the window, nose pointed to the heavens as if a disgusting smell lingers beneath as he observes workers on the factory floor below. Right within his sight the furnaceman, Tommy Turton, toils unaware and, dragging on a heavy steel chain, suspended from girders above, he manfully hauls open a massive cast-iron furnace door, his face a blaze of red and orange when he secures the chain on a hook alongside the raging inferno. 6ft 6ins of solid brawn, shirt sleeves rolled up to his elbows he leans into intolerable temperatures plunging lengthy furnacing tongs into rolling flames and hauling out a heavy, white-hot, metal slab. Resting it on the mill floor he draws himself upright, running a muscular arm along his forehead, mopping rivulets of sweat from his brow on a grubby shirt sleeve, suddenly catching sight of the inquisitive face peering at him from the window above. Clearly agitated by the critical surveillance of a man only recently his equal, he quietly simmers and, angrily hoisting the slab, he pivots, swinging it across the air and bringing it to rest on a metal fore plate in front of nearby rolls handing over the process to the roller, Charlie Thwaites, and his five-man team for completion.

A mere runt of a man, legs bowed by long years of bearing heavy weights, grubby sweat towel knotted at his throat, a huge cloth cap overhangs his forehead, soiled clothing hangs, loosely, against his puny frame, but while Charlie is physically looked down upon by most, in work terms he is a man on a pedestal. A man commanding deep respect from both management and workforce for his skills and expertise, as he mixes genially with both, passing it on to the next generation. Sweating profusely, he grips the metal plate in long, thin tongs guiding it through the hot rolls and barking instructions to the furnaceman simultaneously turning screws, adjusting the rolls and bringing the slab to completion to exact specifications. A scintillating display, red-hot scale flies through the gloom, penetrating clothing, slipping inside work boots and embedding in the skin beneath, but, echoing across the heavily-burdened air, ribald jokes, raucous laughter and camaraderie lighten the load. Between 'heats' copious amounts of salt water quenches thirsts and replaces fluids lost in perspiration.

Sipping from the lid of a metal mashing can, Tommy winks at colleagues, a satisfied smirk on his face while meaningfully tossing his head in the direction of the office window above and loudly delivering a snippet of gossip sufficient to whet the appetite of all within earshot. Intrigued, my father hurries down the nearby stairway a ponderous expression on his face when a cloak of silence immediately falls over the huddled group on the shop floor and a distinct air of mystery surrounds them as he turns to go.

Icy blasts blowing, a group of desperate unemployed wait by the gates of Neepsend Steel and Tool enviously watching their departure at the end of the morning shift, some with faces thrust deep into spread newspapers, telling of troubles brewing in far-off lands, others wistfully peering into the infernal environment of the rolling mill as the afternoon shift bends to their labours.

Driven by exaggerated visions, my father later takes an unusual step, and two things happen in conjunction bringing dire consequences. Lace curtains twitch on Thirza Street at the unusual sound of determined footsteps emerging from a darkened passageway. Faces pressed close to the window, curious onlookers peer into the evening mist intrigued as to why their neighbour is uncharacteristically venturing out on a Saturday night. Perpendicular body swathed in a long, worsted coat, gloved hand anchoring a smart trilby hat to his head, gathering wind lifting his coat tails, my father swaggers round the bend into Wood Street under critical gaze. Furtively cuddling in the shaded doorway of Lingards hardware store, a courting couple stirs bitter memories, spurring him on and, progressing at speed along Langsett Road, he weaves amongst kindred travellers, ringing tread mingling with the steady drone of a lighted tram making its way towards Hillsborough Corner.

Guided by the moon's faint light and an occasional street lamp he hurries through the greyness towards the sprawling stone building of Hillsborough Barracks, tiers of huge, arched and rectangular windows striding along its frontage, roof furnished with battlements. Topped by spiked iron railings, a low stone wall gives way to a cobbled drive disappearing beneath a stone arch leading to the barrack square, and in its curved shadow he stands awhile, bracing himself for what is to come. Drawing out a huge, snow-white, handkerchief he loudly clears his nose and, pensively reconnoitring, finally makes hasty progress over tram tracks towards a tall, angular building of chunky stone opposite. Riotous sounds of merriment escaping from a large casement window, he pauses in dull light falling across the pavement and, tentatively rising on tiptoe, peers over its partially frosted pane, witnessing a sight almost sending him reeling in disgust. Peering from a gently swinging sign, protruding from the corner of the Queens public house, Queen Victoria appears to share his disapproval, her neck held in the vice-like grip of a crinkly ruff. Face solemn under her stern gaze he loiters, struggling to resist natural urges impelling him to run from the place, but, peeling off leather gloves, pointlessly flicking one over his immaculate coat, he makes unnecessary adjustments to the neat Windsor knot at his throat, nudging it from side to side and eventually returning it to the self-same spot between two stiff peaks of a white starched collar. Preparing for entry, he lifts his trilby hat from his head, sweeping the palm of his hand over hair laid flat beneath a layer of Brylcreem and replacing it, shuffles it around until two flimsy feathers, secured to a silk ribbon running around its rim, lie precisely in line with his right shoulder. Pulling on his gloves he points his nose to the heavens, raises himself to his full height and, pushing wide double swing doors, makes a grand entrance. An imposing figure, clutching a coat lapel in each gloved hand, he stands inside the doorway searching a sea of faces curiously returning his gaze through palls of cigarette smoke.

Crude exchanges, loud guffawing and meaningful sniggers offending delicate senses he surveys his surroundings through jaundiced eyes. Empty glasses bear witness to copious beer consumption, overflowing ashtrays to continuous smoking. An oasis of calm amongst the mayhem, two elderly gentlemen sit on stools either side of an ash-strewn hearth, heads folded in quiet contemplation. Firelight playing along craggy profiles, one speaks while the other respectfully listens and, in quiet moments, each lifts a bevelled pint pot from the mantelpiece, sipping genteelly and gazing thoughtfully into the fire as if seriously considering the matter under discussion. Close by, a grubby figure in an obvious state of intoxication, lolls carelessly on a chair beside a glass strewn table, a trembling hand attempting to guide a cigarette to his lips, another holding a pint of ale. Head swaying, he attempts to locate his mouth with the precariously wobbling glass but beer spills over its rim. Glistening in the gaslight it dribbles along his chin and down his scrawny neck, coming to rest on a grubby white silk scarf loosely folded at his throat. Cherub faces, peering up at him from wrought iron legs beneath the table, bear a strange resemblance because the man looks innocent in his drunkenness, his face wreathed in a silly, alcoholic grin when he struggles to return the glass to the table. Clumsily stubbing out his cigarette he fishes around in a worn jacket pocket, eventually drawing out a tiny metal tin and flicks open its lid. Nipping a pinch of snuff between finger and thumb, his arm sways uncontrollably in his attempt to thrust a pinch up each nostril, some scattering down the front of his clothing. An explosive sneeze catapulting a damp, brown spray into the air, my father catches its full blast and, rearing backwards, he gapes in horror at the perpetrator, wiping a dark trail of snuff from beneath stained nostrils with a grubby piece of rag. Drawing out his own pristine handkerchief, he wafts loose brown powder from his clothing and makes a swift half-turn in his urgent need to leave, but the tinkling of a ramshackle piano stops him dead in his tracks.

Searching the thickening haze of cigarette smoke, his eyes immediately fall on my tiny figure, perched on a faded piano stool in a dingy recess by the fire, my every smiling contour lit by flickering flames, feet rhythmically tapping on the wooden floor as strains of 'My Old Man Says Follow the Van' sends the room into a frenzy of wild activity. A motley choir of raucous voices reverberate around the walls, feet pound the floor, bodies sway but there is no Mozart, Handel or Haydn to soothe his soul, only a medley of crude music hall songs battering his eardrums and offending his delicate senses. Clamping a hand against each ear he attempts to shut out the wild cacophony but, struggling to his feet, the inebriated man alongside begins bouncing around to the pulsating rhythm, legs splayed, clogged feet pounding the floor. Taking to the aisles, some dance drunkenly, occasionally pausing to gulp from glasses of ale. Amidst the flurry a scattering of women take to their feet, grinning, squealing and offering an occasional glimpse of knee-length underwear as they dance the can-can until the music fades and the room erupts in banging of fists on table tops and enthusiastic yelling for more. Glazed eyes fixed on the scene, my father is paralysed with rage, but catching sight of a familiar group huddled around a table at the far end of the room his jaw drops, upright stance visibly collapses at the sight of underlings from work smugly staring in his direction, nudging one another meaningfully while wetting throats parched from yelling for an encore. A deafening rendition of 'Goodnight Irene' bringing the exciting evening to a close, I bow and curtsey in pivotal fashion acknowledging the enthusiastic response, face wreathed in a wide grin, but, catching sight of my ashen-faced father, my legs crumble, face assumes a sickly pallor and I feel a desperate need to flee to the outside toilet in order to empty the contents of my churning stomach. Neck craned above the jostling throng, my father is clearly distinguishable and, eyes locking, we both freeze, but with a sudden indignant thrust of his head in my direction he struts, furiously, into the night.

Legs trembling, I battle my way home, a maelstrom of wild thoughts swirling around in my head and desperate to seek the comfort of Harry's arms, urgently stumble over the threshold, but instantly slumping against the door jamb I gape at the sight of Harry and Ellen in the throes of a bitter argument. A flood of desperate tears escaping, I watch Ellen's bony finger wagging close to Harry's nose, her face waxen, mood black as the night. Transfixed by the horror of it all, I stare helplessly, Harry's bloodshot eyes and belligerent expression sending a familiar warning that he has consumed sufficient alcohol to render him incapable of rational thought. Long experience has taught me that alcohol tends to work on his brain in two ways making him a Jekyll and Hyde character, sometimes sending him home in giddy mood so that he torments to the point of frustration, at others bringing out the worst when he vents his anger in fits of wild fury.

Troubles of the world bearing down on his shoulders trivial incidents take on gigantic proportions, slight disagreements invite aggression, but, whichever way the wind blows, I have learned to handle him with kid gloves when he drinks to excess. Frighteningly, a steely look of determination tells me he is in extremely awkward mood as he blatantly challenges Ellen and, desperately clinging to the door jamb, I support my own quivering frame, silently praying his mood will subside. One elbow precariously propped on the edge of the piano, his body swaying, I know drink has washed away all sense of rationality. Moving jerkily, he wrenches a spent cigarette from his lips leans forward and as if aiming a dart at a dartboard, closes one eye, lining the stub up with the fire grate, and eventually launches it into the flames.

He clumsily draws out an old suitcase from the side of the piano and immediately I realise I am watching the sequel to an earlier argument. Helplessly rooted to the spot, I watch his unsteady progress towards the back door, a draught of freezing air sneaking in as he wrenches it wide. Peering into the misty greyness beyond, sheer desperation drives me in his direction and I cling to his jacket tails in an urgent bid to prevent his departure, but he clumsily shakes me free. In sheer blind panic, I fall to my knees, but, common sense impeded, he steps over the threshold, treading a clumsy drunken path down the back yard. Knowing things have reached the point of no return, I lean forward helplessly watching from the doorway his retreat into the shadows. Slumping to the floor, I lay there, body heaving with desperate sobs. Following naturally warm instincts, Ellen crouches alongside throwing her arms around my shoulders and trying to explain, but hurriedly flinging away her arm, I scuttle for the stairway. Rudely disturbed, Audrey Mary screams at my hasty entrance into the bedroom and throughout my careless packing, frantically resists attempts to lift her from the comfort of her warm crib, in a state of drowsiness, and Ellen looks numb with shock on my return to the kitchen, a screaming, writhing baby cradled in one arm, roughly tied bundle under the other, suitcase swinging from my fingers. Face a pale shade of grey, she appears on the brink of collapse and, concerned, I struggle towards her, instinctively planting a gentle kiss on her pallid cheek. Audrey Mary pressed between us she squeezes us tight and we both shed bitter tears of regret.

Mentally and physically burdened, I struggle with my heavy load down the cobbled yard and through the gloom of the blackened passageway, but hearing the upward drag of the sash window alongside, I can't resist a final sideways glance. Ellen's lined, tear-stained face thrust out into the night, I know she will be relieved at the sight of a lit cigarette glowing further down the hill and Harry's shadowy form leaning against a lamp standard, suitcase resting on the cobbles at his feet. Bringing the window down with a resigned thud, Ellen disappears from our lives, but I know she won't sleep tonight, wondering where our stupid, impulsive move will lead us.

CHAPTER SIX
STORM CLOUDS GATHER

The sharp rap of stone hitting glass appears to have rudely awakened my father because he looks dishevelled and deeply concerned, flinging open the bedroom window and leaning over the sill far enough for me to see that he is in his long johns. Squinted eyes, pink and swollen, he rightly looks aggrieved, peering down the line of his nose at us, standing forlorn in the darkness as Audrey Mary's screams ring, hollow, across the silence of the night. Pleadingly, I meet his curious gaze and slamming shut the window he swiftly disappears from view, relief sweeping over me when I hear him struggling with rusting bolts. Hastily donned clothing in disarray, hair tousled, he appears in the open doorway instantly wrenching Audrey Mary from my grasp, but faced with the stranger giving off dangerous signals she violently resists, screaming and frantically waving her arms in my direction. My father is clearly distressed but footsteps hurriedly descending the stairway, my mother arrives in the kitchen in an anxious state. Greying hair tucked beneath a mesh hairnet, long flannelette nightdress flowing, she immediately takes control swiftly lifting a startled Audrey Mary into her arms, stunning her into silence. Shaking her head in disgust, she casts a scathing glance over her shoulder before swiftly disappearing upstairs but her 'told you so' expression says it all. In his drink-induced boldness, Harry is already taking liberties, precariously leaning over the doorstep and depositing suitcases on the kitchen floor. My father appears about to implode. A firm hand clamped across his mouth, his red cheeks inflate as a balloon in a seeming bid to prevent hurtful, intractable words escaping when Harry slumps against the door jamb a rich combination of beer and tobacco drifting from his helpless form. Standing four-square in front of him my father beats an open palm with a clenched fist in his helplessness but the heel of a foot impatiently hammering on the bedroom floor above sends a warning. Ruefully shaking his head in my direction, he follows the unspoken command and I can almost feel his pain as he slams the door behind him, inflicting the weight of his anger on every rising stair tread.

Loud snoring breaking the silence. Harry sleeps the deep sleep of the inebriated lying beside me in my old attic bedroom, but I draw no comfort from the familiar: the moon's hazy face, long keeping me company and making me feel safe throughout childhood, occasional faint twinkling star finding its way through the mist to enchant me through teenage years. The split-second sighting of a lone bat appears synonymous with those fleeting years and lying awake in the darkness; I savour it all for the last time. Throughout the long night, muddled thoughts prevent sleep and by the time shades of early morning begin creeping across the heavily-laden sky, I instinctively know which road to take. Nudging a reluctant Harry into life, I tiptoe down the short flight of stairs to the landing below, creaking stair treads irritatingly shadowing my progress into the front bedroom. Stealthily creeping towards a large dressing table drawer alongside the double bed, I gently lift out a cocoon of warm blankets, taking a final look at my sleeping parents before leaving. 'Shushing' softly in Audrey Mary's ear, I choke back tears, hurrying down the precariously twisting stairway to meet a sober Harry at the front door, a large, bulky bundle tucked beneath his arm, suitcase in each hand.

Footsteps echoing across early morning greyness, we walk aimlessly beneath a leaden sky, a chill wintry wind blowing. Parkwood Springs no more than a shadowy scene slowly emerging on the far horizon, my old school a ghostly apparition in the light of a pale rising sun; the haunting hoot of a distant train evokes a desperate sense of loneliness, but the deed is done now. Thin trails of smoke, curling from multiple domestic chimneys, signal the beginning of another Neepsend day and under the puzzled gaze of early morning travellers we come to rest, our backs towards the Don wall. Unsettled by her rude awakening, disturbed by the morning's icy blasts Audrey Mary tosses, turns and whimpers within the mound of bedding and, not a word passing between us, Harry and I struggle with the guilt of inflicting our desperate situation on an innocent child. Lifting her into my arms I attempt a soothing lullaby in her ear, desperate sobs marring the words, but soon the gentle lapping of the Don lulls her into a restless sleep.

Church bells tolling, a steady stream of people, dressed in Sunday best, begin making their way to a squat church alongside the Roscoe Picture Palace to pray, pungent aroma of moth balls drifting from their person, voices soft and reverential out of respect for the Sabbath. However, enthused by their fervent belief in a Supreme Being they almost lift the roof of the church, lustily praising the Lord in song. In damp, cramped houses, people tune into services weekly relayed over the air waves, but, as the hymns of ages promise succour and support for the needy, tell of a magical resurrection and a wonderful afterlife, our faith in The Almighty is already fast fading with deteriorating weather conditions.

A shallow sleep leaves Audrey Mary in a contrary mood and, insisting on demonstrating faltering new steps, she delays progress around damp streets bathed in a poisonous fog, her wails of protest possibly contributing to the negative responses to numerous requests for a place to stay. Nose red and runny, face sullen, she stumbles at a distance, finally depositing herself on freezing cold cobblestones, noisily demanding attention. A sudden squall washing the streets she awkwardly kicks and screams when I haul her into my arms, scuttling for cover beneath a gloomy passageway on Capel Street, but, though a fine shaft of sunlight finally struggles through the mist and the sharp shower ceases, Audrey Mary's dark mood refuses to lift. First demanding to be carried, the next to be set down she finally tires of both, wailing miserably and again throwing herself in a crumpled heap on cobblestones outside the Royal Infirmary. Mindful of their own child-rearing days the more tactful turn a blind eye and cock a deaf ear, others mutter words of sympathy for Audrey Mary, viewing Harry and I with suspicion. Shaking their heads, in know-it-all fashion, a group of like-minded busybodies huddle together, casting occasional caustic comments into the air and, under their critical gaze, we attempt to pacify, but there is no consoling Audrey Mary because she is distraught at our pointless wanderings.

Tired of battle she finally concedes defeat in a cradle of blankets tucked in the crook of my arm as church bells peel mid-day. The early morning rising setting the tone of Audrey Mary's mood for the day, she whines miserably throughout the afternoon trek up the mountainous slopes to Parkwood Springs, around numerous houses in the valley bottom and, interest in new walking skills fast fading, she perches on Harry's extended forearm, one arm draped around his neck, head resting on his shoulder, mouth furiously sucking on her thumb for comfort, eyes gradually closing.

Daylight fast fading, storm clouds gather overhead and despondency turns to horror when a torrential downpour washes the streets. Urgently racing into a narrow shop doorway along Infirmary Road, Harry and I peer into the blackness beyond and, an occasional street light sending a fine incandescence around its own circumference, the sprawling Royal Infirmary is soon no more than rows of dimly lit windows seen through a blanket of rain and dense fog. Anxiously scanning the jet sky, we reluctantly accept our inevitable fate. Two suitcases forming a barrier against rain threatening to spill over the thin wedge of a doorstep, we create a makeshift cradle in the corner of the doorway and sobbing uncontrollably, I tuck a restless Audrey Mary into its folds rocking her gently until her screams become a whimper and finally cease. Settling alongside her on the concrete floor, our backs against a large plate glass window, Harry and I huddle close, searching angry skies for signs of abatement, but way above Upperthorpe, jagged lightning issues a stark warning. Zig-zagging across the black sky, it periodically lights the darkness, casting a mass of shadowy buildings in silhouette on its downward journey and cutting across the pitched roof of the Royal Infirmary, makes silver the pouring rain. Peals of thunder rumble across the leaden skies, exploding overhead and cruelly startling Audrey Mary. Instantly upright, she screams shrilly, arms outstretched in a frantic bid for rescue but, though wrapped in a warm cocoon of blankets in the cradle of my lap, she still trembles with fear. Nature's grand overture gradually becomes a wild orchestral played by terrifying elements. Caught in the momentary glow of a lightning flash the ghostly face of the Infirmary clock tells us it's midnight but Audrey Mary still lies awake, her head tucked beneath the covers in a bid to hide from the terrors of the night.

Overnight the storm gathers pace and in a frenzy of wild activity lightning flashes light the sky, thunder bolts explode overhead, torrential rain lashes shop windows, bounces off cobblestones, gushes down hollow drainpipes and, gurgling noisily, tumbles down grates along the edge of roads. Blustery winds shake wooden shutters, metal shop signs swing wildly from rusting chains and a terrifying finale to nature's masterpiece, a series of mighty thunderclaps bring things to a sudden dramatic end. Black clouds scudding on the wind, the arc of a pale sun finally peers through, barely lighting streets refreshed by the night's spring clean.

Public facilities and occasional use of an outside toilet our only means of preserving dignity, five days of trekking through wind, rain and sleet in a fruitless search for a roof over our heads leave us bedraggled and devoid of hope. Thin crescent of a moon and the occasional gas lamp lighting the night, fine shafts of pale sunlight barely warming the day, we pass by crocodile queues of dejected people waiting by the gas works to replenish dwindling fuel stocks. Strategically positioned on a corner outside the Farfield Inn, a young boy keeps a furtive eye on behalf of an illegal gambling ring, tossing coins on the hump of Hillfoot Bridge, and he is growing wary of our regular passing. Time on their hands, huddled groups of unemployed also wile away the days and there is a hopeless feel about the place. Many factory gates closed now, there is no army of marching men to witness our misery, no open doorways through which to watch awhile their labours and break the monotony of endless hours or from which to warm ourselves in the escaping heat of roaring furnaces, because the recession is biting deep.

No order to our days, we pointlessly roam around the streets of Neepsend, sometimes climbing the station steps to lean over the railings and watch trains carrying others through daily lives or coming to rest on a wooden form outside the Royal Infirmary where brash fascias offer a multitude of goods and services. A colourful oasis, distinctive hoardings trumpet the benefits of Pears soap, Bisto or Ovaltine.

A clear sign of desperate times, some tread a furtive path to the shop with three brass balls hanging above the doorway in order to, sometimes reluctantly, surrender often highly treasured possessions in exchange for cash to see them through the bad times. Mocking attempts at silent entry a massive iron bell, hanging just inside the doorway, loudly jangles alerting the world to their arrival. Money short, many flit in and out of shops at speed, concentrating solely on necessities and, between numerous vain attempts to find a place to stay, we wile away the hours amongst the hustle and bustle of everyday life. Idly passing the time we sometimes peer, longingly, in shop windows, wistfully eyeing tempting displays out of reach. In the butcher's window succulent sausages hang from metal hooks, bloodied trays of offal rest in the shade of striped awning and, straddled across the pavement in front of the baker's shop next door, a giant sandwich board portrays a huge, jolly man in bakers' whites holding a steaming pie in an outstretched hand. Mouth-watering cakes and buns, set on fancy cake stands at the front of the window, taunt us daily but what little money we have is dwindling and, Audrey Mary our priority, we first tend to her needs, neglecting our own. Nevertheless, she is fretting at the discomfort of our nomadic lifestyle, but, suddenly, our dire situation becomes fraught with danger. Lying still and unresponsive in the fold of my arm, Audrey Mary whimpers constantly throughout the endless journey around streets bathed in a poisonous mist, but raging temperature, runny nose, swiftly spreading rash suggests urgency and, in a state of blind panic, we flee to the gates of the Royal Infirmary. Complications arising from a bout of measles have already set in and, stubbornly refusing to respond to treatment, Audrey Mary is weakening to the point of no return. Lights going out in my world, I watch her fade and by the time darkness falls over a bleak, freezing Neepsend, she peacefully slips from our lives.

A black cloud descending I lose all control, ranting wildly, throwing accusations at Harry and blaming myself until my energy is spent. In my extreme anguish, I resort to wild imaginings, telling myself she is only sleeping to compensate for long nights catnapping in shop doorways and that morning will find her again safely cradled in my arms, but, curtains closing around her bed now, I know she has forever gone from our lives. Repressed by masculine pride, Harry stands silent, facial muscles twitching, lips trembling, face white as the starched sheet on which the tiny corpse lies and it's clear he is suffering.

The burden of guilt weighing heavy we walk slowly down stark, white-washed corridors, heads folded, tears streaming in our unbearable grief, leaving behind a part of us on that hospital ward, but the distance forged between us is almost tangible and sadly, the one thing that had so firmly bound us together is now secretly tearing us apart.

CHAPTER SEVEN
THE FAMILY WAY

Courtesy of a local landlord a tiny furnished rented property on Thirza Street gives us a new start but, overlooking the front window of my childhood home, it stirs bitter memories, rubbing salt into open wounds, and the empty bedroom only highlights the fact that there is no child to occupy it. Each day, a care-worn face pressed against the window opposite, my mother tracks my every move, her shocked expression telling me she is dreadfully concerned at the drastic change in me. Weight plummeting, face etched with misery, eyes red and swollen from much crying, it's clear the weight of the world bears down on my young shoulders, a spark extinguished from my life. The pull of my first born too strong to resist, regular solitary climbs up the slopes towards Walkley Cemetery only increase my misery but I am not yet ready to let go.

Swung wide, old wrought iron gates seem to mockingly invite me in but, once inside, a winged angel, rearing from a stone plinth at the head of the tiny grave, appears to welcome me with open arms, a gravestone inscribed with a heartfelt message, partially hidden beneath a fine covering of gently falling snow, telling of another lost child. Suffering writ large in their faces, I share the anguish of strangers wandering around the cemetery, some with bunches of flowers laid across their arms or lovingly tending inscribed urns standing testament to their abiding pain and suffering and, the strange aura and eerie silence does nothing to lift my misery on advancing through the grey morning.

Pausing, I watch a kneeling form tidying a loved one's plot, placing a token of remembrance and planting a kiss on the headstone before walking away, head folded. Highlighting my own loss, upright crosses, simple gravestones, majestic memorials bear similar heart-rending messages of love and loss and, ingrained with the dirt of ages, some tip into sunken earth. Tall stone and marble figures rise majestically above dark, angular vaults, blank eyes staring towards eternity through a growing cascade of snow soon settling, as a cape, over their shoulders. Boldly engraved with the names of the more eminent in life, they serve as a lasting reminder of worldly wealth and importance but, tucked between, desolate pauper plots mark the passing of the poor and humble and, lying beneath their shadows, their lowly position in life lingers in death.

Bleak and oppressive, the graveyard tells its stories. Inscribed marble urns stand on long-neglected gravestones, reminding of people lost in wars long gone, succumbing to various epidemics or dying in tragic circumstances over the years but, occasionally, a carefully-placed bunch of fresh flowers tells the world a surviving friend or relative still remembers. Over the years, Sheffield's corrosive industrial dust and grime has eaten away at inscriptions, indecipherable remnants rendering anonymous those lying beneath. Virgin snow shifting beneath my feet, I make my way to a tiny plot in a far corner of the cemetery and, newly-dug graves along the way soon someone's final resting place, I hurry by, eyes averted. Knee bent against snow-covered earth I place a tiny posy of flowers on a freshly created mound of soil and, sobbing bitterly, lean against a tall, naked oak keeping my first-born company awhile. It's a harrowing journey home, leaving her lying beneath the first snow of winter.

Guilt and regret gradually driving a deeper wedge between us, Harry and I are as strangers, unwillingly thrust under one roof. Nevertheless, renewed interest in politics, active engagement in various movements and continuing search for work, Harry's life is a frenzy of activity and there is too much going on in his life for scars of bereavement to be visible. Regular contact with old friends lifting his spirits, liquid sustenance drowns his sorrows, eases the humiliation and boredom of life on the dole and drains resources. Even the fire in the grate fails to warm a home, merely providing shelter from the elements and, my own family long estranged, it's a lonely life and Harry's interest in things domestic is non-existent. Fuelled by close proximity, simmering hatred between my father and Harry manifests itself in many ways and, unknown to either, evasive actions of comical proportions secretly entertain. Whenever the clatter of clogged feet and tapping of highly-polished brogues signal their simultaneous arrival onto Thirza Street from dark passageways, faces appear at steamy windows, keen to witness the familiar ritual designed for each to outwit the other. Feigning ignorance of Harry's emergence, my father deliberately hovers in the shadows, biding time in a bid to avoid confrontation. By way of diversion he carefully examines immaculate clothing, flicks away every imaginary speck of dust with a gloved hand and, lifting each foot in turn, rubs a gleaming toe cap along the back of each opposite trouser leg. Fiddling with the brim of his trilby hat he pointlessly checks it sits squarely on his head and, deliberately stalling, reaches into his waistcoat pocket bringing out the family heirloom. Drawing out a neatly folded handkerchief from the top pocket of his jacket he shakes it loose, breathing heavily on its pristine face and carefully polishing the glass, with the sole purpose of forcing Harry to make the first move. Carefully folding the handkerchief, he slips it back in place until only three neat peaks protrude but a stunted shadow still lies stubbornly across the cobblestones opposite. Knowing my father is tied to daily routine, Harry goads, and appearance shabby by comparison, he casually leans against the wall by the front window whistling a jaunty tune. Reaching deep into a worn jacket pocket he brings out a cigarette-rolling machine, rusty tobacco tin containing slivers of tobacco salvaged from previous stubs, a box of matches sliced down the middle for thrift and a slim packet of cigarette papers. Slowly he rolls a cigarette, tapping each end against the top of the tin to compact the tobacco, finally slipping it between his lips. Striking a wafer-thin match against the rough brick wall he shelters the flimsy flame with a cupped hand, carefully applying it to the cigarette and puffing rapidly until it flares into life. Lazily drawing in nicotine, he visibly relaxes at the first inhalation and, looking skywards, slowly opens and closes his mouth, releasing perfectly formed smoke rings into the murky air. Impatiently tapping his foot against the cobblestones, my father again withdraws the timepiece, anxiously checking the time, but finally forced to admit defeat he swaggers along Thirza Street in defiant mode. Jauntily hurrying in his wake, Harry finally overtakes him on the turn of Wood Street, and curtains falling back in place; neighbours merely laugh at the predictability of it all.

My father thinks he can't be seen – his face pressed against the lace curtain opposite – but I fear he would be livid to learn Harry and I have finally married in a hasty ceremony without need of his consent. Still, we are unlikely to hang out banners in the face of his fierce disapproval. A necessary piece of paper and mere formality; the gold ring simply tells the world I am forbidden territory but does nothing to heal the rift between us, because little has changed. Harry's firm belief in male superiority and entitlement to personal freedom, matched by an equally strong belief in a woman's duty to forfeit hers and commit solely to drudgery, he is a chauvinist and the scales of marriage tip overwhelmingly in his favour. My pleadings failing to curb his wanderings, he goes his way, and I am tied to domesticity.

Nevertheless, I have learned to live with the situation and things are beginning to run more smoothly. Indeed. Nellie Schofield has become a common sight on Thirza Street and my parents must have noted, with some concern, the regularity of her visits. One on a freezing cold winter morning, one at the end of a beautiful spring day, and one at the height of summer, and my mother's eagle eyes will surely have noted the recent gradual swelling at my waist, concerned there is barely a chink of light between each birth. For certain, my father will be furious at the prospect of our poverty existence worsening. In fact, over recent weeks, studying the wisdom of reproducing at such a pace, common sense and constant daily struggle has already driven me to a determined decision to speak to Harry with a view to making this the final addition to our rapidly growing family.

Audrey Mary's death has left a gaping void in the family but I gain great comfort from the fact that a part of her lingers in siblings, familiar mannerisms and facial expressions keeping her close. Poverty, however, has become increasingly stressful and, forced to swallow my pride, I reluctantly search second-hand shops, accept cast-off clothing from neighbours in my determination to make sure my boys don't go without. Flouting the law, I take in washing, earning a few extra coppers to eke out scant income, but the risks are great and fear ever present. Even the old bucket pram has seen the best of its days but Michael, my new born, snuggled at one end, Steven perched at the other, feet swinging, Peter toddling alongside, we tread a weekly path to the cemetery, gradually acquainting the living with the dead and bringing Audrey Mary back into the fold.

In the midst of domestic strife, deteriorating local events cast an even darker shadow, and government plans to cut pitiful dole payments meeting fierce opposition, disillusioned masses restlessly mill around the streets of Sheffield venting their spleen in, often violent, confrontations with authority. The uprisings sometimes cruelly quelled, things are spiralling out of control and what began as discussion amongst a few has finally been brought to public attention. Caught in the excitement and challenge of it all, Harry is becoming a stranger, immersing himself in local battles and keeping abreast of political events.

Each day, troubles at home and abroad grow more ominous, dampening my enthusiasm for the fact that Harry has finally found work! A conductor on the trams, a smart new uniform finally becomes his passport to respectability. In black serge trousers and matching jacket, thick leather straps criss-crossing his puny chest, a ticket machine hangs at one side of his waist, punch the other and the shiny peak of a flat-topped hat overhanging his nipped nose, he flaunts his authority, cocking a snook at my father whenever he boards. Renewed enthusiasm for life, he is a different man, introducing us to his world and larger than life characters met on his travels. Recognising their entertainment value, he skilfully weaves hilarious stories around each one, his bellicose laughter, my deep-throated chuckle and childish giggles encouraging often much-exaggerated recollection.

Employment, however, does nothing to curb his interest in politics and drink. In fact, it serves little other purpose than to validate his right to freedom, and money to spend freely in the Farfield. Family income mainly earned by his own efforts, he guards every penny, paring my spending to the bone so that we still live on the breadline, but every day, poverty is falling further down my worry list because international events are becoming extremely serious. Talk of war in the air, people are nervous and, troubles edging closer to home, powerful maternal instincts make me fear for my offspring. In quiet moments dwelling on terrifying scenarios, my imagination runs riot and exaggerated visions of explosions rocking the planet, fires raging around the world, complete extinction of life itself, wear me down. Intense paranoia impacts badly on all our lives and I am bemused by my sudden mood changes, but, daily sending me scurrying over the back yard to empty the contents of my stomach over the toilet pan, familiar symptoms issue a warning. Another pregnancy. The prospect of bringing yet another innocent child into dire poverty in an ever more turbulent world weighs heavy and, plagued with uncertainty, I hold my secret close but common sense dictates I consider my next move as a matter of urgency.

A shadowy figure darting through dense fog, I hurry alongside the Don wall, head and shoulders draped in the folds of a long, black shawl, tapping footsteps muted by a light tread and buried in the hoot of a train chugging along the distant track. Slanting through thick cloud, a pale shaft of moonlight barely pierces the darkness and, flitting eyes scouring the shadows of Anlaby Street, I stand awhile listening for approaching footsteps beyond the water's rush before hurrying on. Coming to halt outside a tiny house close by the weir, I search the night and, finally dipping in, a swift curtsey, slip a folded note through the grids of a cellar grate.

Over subsequent sleepless nights and tormented days a multitude of conflicting emotions wash over me and, bearing the brunt of my anxiety, innocent children are clearly bewildered by this newly impatient me angrily responding to shrill voices and shrieking laughter during their childish play. But soon the long-awaited visitor arrives at my door. Cautiously lifting the corner of a faded lace curtain at the kitchen window, I see an anxious face looking back. Captured in faint moonlight, a shabby young girl shifts restlessly from foot to foot, blowing into cupped hands exposed to the cold night air. Pouched lips spreading in a weak smile, row of bulging teeth readily identify her as an offspring of Nancy Chapman, oversized coat with bulky turned-up hem and sleeves, confirm that poverty continues to dog the family line. Clearly agitated by the covert nature of her errand, Emma Chapman shuffles awkwardly on the spot, slipping her hand under a pointed pixie bonnet to furiously scratch a mass of tousled hair as I open the door. Urgently thrusting a crumpled note in my direction, she immediately turns, scampering back across the back yard, and the clap of oversized Wellington boots flapping against scrawny legs tells me she is racing along the passageway. Indecision and uncertainty dogs every subsequent day and, forfeiting sleep, time drags until the day of reckoning.

Cowed and shifty, I venture, almost on tiptoe, on a repeat of that earlier journey, shoulders hunched, quivering fingers clutching the same black shawl to my face. Casting furtive glances around darkened streets, I ward off the unexpected, and the shadowy outline of a snaking queue on the far side of Hillfoot Bridge prompts me to urgently dip my head over the Don wall, shielding my face from prying eyes as it approaches. Caught in a shaft of pale moonlight falling across the waves, a tired, haunted face looks back and, the steady drone of the tram alerting me to its imminent arrival, I follow its lighted reflection, monitor its monotonous sound until it fades into the distance. Eyes warily flitting, I scuttle into the darkness of Anlaby Street, lingering in its shadows at every sound but, caught in a faint beam of light escaping from a partially opened door close by the weir, an inquisitive face peers into the darkness. Courage failing, I make tentative progress in her direction and am about to turn back when a grasping hand reaches into the night hauling me, unceremoniously, indoors without warning.

Swiftly closing the door behind me Nancy Chapman hurries to the window, cautiously lifting the corner of a thick brown curtain and scouring the street for possible witnesses to my arrival. A single gas mantle lights the dingy room, flickering firelight sends Nancy's short, rounded form darting around distempered walls as elongated shadows, as she flits between kitchen and living room bringing with her the tools of her illegal trade and introducing the pungent odour of carbolic soap. In short-sleeved floral blouse and long black skirt long, strands of mousey fine hair fall against plump cheeks as she works at speed, draping a thick blanket over a chaise longue and covering it with a thinning, oft-bleached bed sheet. Still to-ing and fro-ing, she finally emerges from the kitchen bearing a huge, matching jug and bowl, placing it on an old wooden sideboard and laying a large white towel alongside. Snuggled in its folds a long, thin knitting needle sends a sinister message and an extended chubby arm directing me towards the chaise longue, Nancy pauses a moment allowing me time for reflection before proceeding, and, her words only highlighting my fears, I feel a desperate urge to escape from the trap of my own making. Blind fear threatening to weaken steely resolve built up over long, sleepless nights half of me is tempted to make an urgent dash for the door but common sense holds me fast and resignedly laying back on the chaise longue, there is no longer any need for words between us.

Waddling across the room Nancy dips into an old gramophone lowering its arm and while a blunt needle squeezes an even older song out of a worn record, I survey the room. Though bare floorboards and old furniture reflect a lifetime of poverty, a whiff of lavender furniture polish and black lead suggests Nancy is house proud in spite of it. Dusky home-pegged rug in front of the hearth conjures visions of her huddled in that dingy, fire-lit, room on a cold winter's evening, an old shawl warding off draughts, chubby fingers weaving multi-coloured strips of old material into a piece of sacking with aid of a wooden peg, whittled to a fine point. Set in a huge oval frame a large photograph hangs from a picture rail close to the ceiling, bearing witness to a long-ago wedding. In long white sequinned dress and lace veil, a small bouquet of flowers clutched against her chest, a solemn young woman with sallow complexion, pouched lips and protruding teeth bear the hallmark of the Chapman clan, suggesting she might be Nancy's mother. Exuding an autocratic air, a handsome hirsute young man stands alongside in dark pin-striped suit, pink carnation pinned to its lapel, snow-white shirt with stiffly starched collar, a black dicky-bow resting against a protruding Adam's apple. A waxed handlebar moustache expertly twirled into a point at either end, neatly shaped goatee beard springing from the chin of a full, rounded face, the same thick, bushy eyebrows suggest it might be her father.

A croaking voice singing, off-key, in accompaniment to the discordant musical rendering of an old music hall song, it seems Nancy is unaffected by the dramatic process of disposing of human life as she begins inserting the crude instrument, expertly probing. Writhing in discomfort, I feel a trickle of warm blood escaping as she drives it home and the enormity of what has just ensued, too difficult to comprehend, a flood of terrifying emotions engulf me and I feel a desperate desire to turn back the clock, reverse the irreversible, but, forcing me to face the brutal truth, a dramatic crimson stain on the sheet beneath me reminds me it had been destined to be a living, breathing addition to our family.

The deed done now, only a cold, gaping void remains and I know that moment of loss will be indelibly etched on my mind. Even Nancy's warning words fail to prepare me for the unexpected whirlwind tearing at body and soul, draining every drop of emotion until I am mentally spent and overcome with remorse. I instinctively know there will be repercussions. In a dazed state I slowly ease myself from the chaise longue, conscience heavily burdened. Carelessly pulling on my coat, tears stream as I drape the long shawl over hair hung limp with perspiration and feel like Judas handing over payment for my wicked deed. A sickening lurch threatening to bring the contents of my stomach upwards, I stumble through a mist of confusion across the back yard a hand clamped firmly across my mouth in a bid to avoid soiling the cobblestones. Blindly staggering, I fall to my knees in the privacy of the toilet and head thrust over the toilet bowl, violently retch and sob with regret.

CHAPTER EIGHT
DARK SHADOWS

Guilt plays havoc with my troubled mind and a ghostly vision in the middle of the night, haunting figment of my imagination throughout the day, my first born constantly reminds me of the deliberate act snuffing out precious life so cruelly denied her. Dark despondent moods affect us all and it's a miserable existence on Thirza Street. In my deeply depressed state, everything bears heavily on my shoulders, troubled thoughts spiral out of control and, abortion tantamount to murder in the eyes of the law, I fancy I see uniformed men at every turn. Forever on guard, I am obsessed with peering around the edge of the curtain afraid of being caught unaware by an authoritative figure rapping on the door and can never relax. Secrecy imperative, just one careless slip of the tongue could see Nancy imprisoned, myself hauled into court to give evidence and, venturing out only when extremely necessary, home has become a prison cell. My patience short, the children weep and wail in the miserable confined space but we are on a treadmill and no amount of Harry's scolding at the inexplicable change in me can lift me from the doldrums.

Neepsend is buzzing. One of Nancy's illegal abortions has gone wrong. Directed to her door, courtesy of a sympathetic grape vine, a desperate young woman has contracted a serious infection and everybody knows that, handcuffed and under police surveillance in a hospital bed, she will be subjected to tremendous pressure to reveal the truth. A cloak of fear is descending because ramifications of a forced confession will be widespread and, where doors were once left open for friends and neighbours to freely enter, keys will automatically turn in locks. Anxious faces will peer around edges of curtains at every dreaded knock on the door, checking their visitor is not wearing a dark uniform with shiny buttons, domed cap with royal insignia. Anonymity protected only by the loyalty of those forming a grapevine, a mutual vow of silence binds them but it is readily recognised that a sick, terrified young woman will find it hard to resist the intense interrogation of the law. Ears to the ground, women of Neepsend wait with bated breath but giant headlines, screaming from a newspaper placard, dash all hopes of a possible reprieve for Nancy – LOCAL WOMAN ARRESTED ON ILLEGAL ABORTION CHARGE.

Overcome with guilt I know that if found guilty Nancy will, for certain, face a prison sentence and that, at her age, it may bring on the end. Subject to Public Censure by court decree the young woman's misdeed will be revealed to the whole city and, publicly named and shamed, her character will be openly torn to shreds, fingers will point in her direction; people will talk in whispers as she passes. Should Nancy succumb to the same pressure to reveal her clients' names, my fate will be the same and I will be forced to carry a huge burden of shame through life. Every aspect of my life laid bare under equally graphic headlines, salacious adjectives will paint my character black and portray me as a wanton killer in order to deter others.

A dark shadow cast over it, the whole family's name will be blackened, my father's pristine character dragged through the mud and visions of uniformed men clamping me in handcuffs and hauling me outdoors, in full view of the neighbours, haunt me night and day. Every waking minute I live in dread of my name being prised from Nancy, of myself being forced into a disloyal confession, Nancy facing an extended sentence and subsequently rotting behind bars because of me.

Unable to singularly carry the weight of guilt, a confession does nothing to lighten it because Harry is incandescent with rage. Caustic comments rolling off his tongue, he vents his rage, lambasting me in sentences punctuated with deeply wounding profanities, when he is unable to find words sufficient to express the depth of his fury. Nevertheless, the law keen in demanding severe penalties for abortion, his anger is understandable and the rift between us has thrown the whole family into further turmoil. Every new day carrying me further into a black hole, I sit dejected by the fire, immediately on rising, hands wringing in despair, mind tortured by the prospect of possible exposure. Shunning parental responsibility, I shout and scream with frustration when childish demands intrude on my private misery and, confused and bewildered, they are becoming subdued and wary in my company. Expression dull and lifeless, moods dark as mists hanging like a funereal shroud over Neepsend, chaos builds around me and, unable to haul me back from the depths, Harry seeks medical help, my whole world finally collapsing on being referred to the dreaded Fir Vale Institution, my children into the care of Herries Road Children's Home in the same grounds.

Despite its name changing from the workhouse and some of its wings converted for care of the poor and mentally ill, Firvale Infirmary still strikes fear into those entering its walls. Set between two rounded stone columns, each topped with a large, cast-iron, lantern to light the way to its door when darkness falls, huge iron gates menacingly draw me in. Tall poplars cast long shadows over a winding pathway edged with colourful nasturtium borders, rain beats upon waving foliage and I cling desperately to Harry as we approach the awesome building rearing its ugly head at the head of the pathway. A frightening testament to a dying age, its ice-cold aura screams of a brutal past and despite its isolation in a deep hollow falling away from Barnsley Road, its presence is felt. Housing the unfortunate, unruly and socially unaccepted the institution has long proved a cross between a prison and sanctuary, a large round-faced clock, set in the girth of an imposing rising spire, menacingly ticking away the tedium for those destined to spend their days inside its walls, keeping a watchful eye over the surrounding area and serving as a warning to those outside whose unruly behaviour might one day see them committed there. Its reputation travelling down the years, the fearsome place has long beckoned the vulnerable into a world of cruelty and degradation. Lives mapped out from birth, many suffering deformities, formed in the womb, face the rejection of society and find the awful place their home. Faced with circumstances beyond their control, others look to its shelter as a last resort, spirits broken by years of poverty and struggle. Cast out in disgrace, unmarried mothers find their way to its door or are forced inside by parents shamed by their human frailties. Though some escaped over the years, many died of exposure unable to survive in the difficult world outside. Defeated, others returned to discover the cold comfort of a roof over their head and bread in their bellies preferable to bitter elements and starvation. Vagrants find their way up the winding driveway in search of a bed for the night, chopping sticks or separating cobbles of coal into various sizes to pay for dubious hospitality in Tramps Row, a basic stone building designed to temporarily accommodate the homeless. Instinct immediately impels me to flee, on arriving at the foot of wide stone steps leading to its door, but I know I am in no fit state to battle alone the black depression dragging me down or cope with the pressures of a life thrown out of kilter and, mentally weakened, I reluctantly succumb, flatly refusing to look back when Harry leaves me in the reception area.

Stripped of personal clothing and draped in sackcloth, my humiliation is captured in a photograph and consigned to the annals of the institution. Highly polished piano, distinguished composers a distant memory, the talented, articulate young girl lost in the sands of time, I am a shadow of my former self. Confusing nurses in dark blue overalls and frilly starched hats, concerning doctors in white coats, stethoscope draped around their necks, with my constant begging for forgiveness and pleading to be allowed to live if I tell the truth, because nobody understands. In my desperately depressed state, guilt is spilling over and I am possibly digging my own grave with my wild, haunted look and curious declarations of unworthiness because, placed under surveillance, it's as if they consider me capable of harming myself or others. Long, dark nights in this dreadful place are frightening, mournful sounds of misery echoing around clinical walls lit only by firelight, winds rustling leaves in the trees outside, flailing branches throwing ghostly caricatures against the window panes making me desperately long for the security and comfort of home. Nightly shadows are as terrifying as the constant daily probing of medical staff in an attempt to source the root of my mental disturbance but their sympathy will no doubt vanish as a puff of smoke should I weaken sufficient to confess. Even the bible calls for an eye in return for an eye but, conscience burdened, mind haunted by images of young children left behind, my mental torment is punishment enough. In my morbid world there is no light, no purpose to life, no end to misery; because the consequences of confession are too terrifying to comprehend, my secret can never be revealed nor conscience eased by its sharing. A new era of government-approved medical interventions in the field of mental illness arriving on the scene, my inexplicable withdrawn state leaves me ripe for experimentation and I fall victim to trials of a new Insulin Shock Therapy treatment. Injected three times daily, a powerful narcotic introduces me to a world of horrific imaginings over which I have no control and, gradually burning up blood sugar, it dramatically plunges, sending my body into shock with dramatic effect. Desperately flailing and threshing around in a state of absolute confusion, eyes rolling, body drenched in sweat, my life is suddenly at risk when I slip into a coma. Urgent withdrawal brings dramatic consequences and immediately on waking I writhe around in the throes of a massive epileptic fit, eyes gaping in bemusement at the world. Yet, instinctively I know nothing can restore my peace of mind while trouble is waiting in the wings.

Nancy has been sentenced to TEN YEARS imprisonment. A bolt from the blue, the shocking news further shakes my unstable world, plunging me even further into the black hole of depression. And. shrinking further from reality, I retire into an impenetrable shell. Paranoid, I anxiously track every movement of medical staff. viewing their every innocent passing glance with suspicion, whispered conversation as idle talk about myself. and tormented by thoughts of impending doom, I have no lust for life. Over troubled days and sleepless nights, conscience tears me apart because, at her age, Nancy will surely never come out alive and I feel I will never survive these endlessly dark days bearing the guilt of her fate and feeling the hand of the law pressing on my shoulder.

Trapped in a waking nightmare, I can never rest and, constantly listening for determined footsteps purposefully striding the corridor outside, I live in fear of the door at the end of the ward swinging wide to reveal an approaching nurse accompanied by a uniformed policeman. Existing in a dark bubble, tortured days turn into weeks, weeks into months, but the year turning now, there has been no official arrival and, a great burden lifting, it appears Nancy has kept her counsel and saved my skin. A chink of light at last shining through the darkness, dormant emotions come to life and the world slowly donning various seasonal colours, home finally appears on the horizon. Nevertheless, shadows of the workhouse forever destined to hang over me, I will never again feel a complete sense of pride. Tarred with the brush of madness, afraid some unseen hand might reach out and haul me back, my feet barely touch the ground as I scuttle away from the workhouse ashamed of my time there. Head bent, I flit in every available shadow towards the door of the Children's Home, a relentless flood of anguished tears escaping when I hug tightly my bewildered children and scamper with them through huge iron gates to freedom. As if a visible badge tells of my existence there, I feel the eyes of the world looking over my shoulder and, head hung low, hollow eyes full of pain, flee for the safety and anonymity of home. The same dark veil of shame hanging over my family, I know it will be hard adjusting to life with this huge stigma wrapped around us

When Nellie hears the news of another pregnancy she is livid and determined to intervene on my behalf, when called on to attend the birth.

Body swathed in a huge mackintosh, woollen hat pressed firmly on her head, knee-length boots tentatively tread virgin snow, and pure determination drives her up the icy slope of Wood Street, Harry firmly in mind. Snow flurries driving across her path, she finally rounds the treacherous curve into Thirza Street and, a trio of excited boys innocently conducting a snowball fight, a stray missile skims the snow at her feet. Childish voices drift from cloistered back yards, festive sounds drift from tinsel-trimmed front rooms and buoyed by the seasonal atmosphere, she softly hums a song of regal birth the world, suddenly a happier place despite its threats.

Sounds of mayhem from a nearby, dimly-lit front window, she pauses, secretly worrying about another imminent birth as she peers in. Carelessly strung from wall to wall, home-made paper chains sway in draughts finding their way through old doors and windows, a beautiful choral rendering of 'Away in a Manger' drifts from an old wireless but indignant boys squabbling, distressed infant demanding attention, a tired voice vainly calls them to order and things are clearly chaotic. Over the years, Nellie has formed a close bond with the family and, rapping sharply on the back door, enters without invitation. Respecting my vain attempts to keep the poverty home clean and tidy, she removes her wet boots just over the threshold and, shuffling her mackintosh from her shoulders, leans into the night, vigorously shaking it over the backyard. Bustling across the kitchen she drapes it over a clothes horse by the hearth, hooks her soaked hat over the end-post and, first task obvious, breaks up the squabbling duo. Helping an indignant Peter into a thick winter coat, she wraps her own long, woollen scarf around his neck as a muffler and, stooping awkwardly, pulls a pair of Wellington boots over his tiny feet. The flat of her hand pressed into the small of his back she ushers him into the night armed with an urgent request for a neighbour to fetch Harry from the Farfield. Scooping the distressed infant from the depths of the old bucket pram, Nellie paces the room rocking her gently until screams fade and she finally concedes defeat in the comfort of her ample bosom as she ushers me up the stairs to await the birth.

When the new born fills the house with lusty screams, both Nellie and I suspect a reincarnation! Identical sprigs of dark hair at intervals springing across her tiny scalp, the tiny infant is a replica of ill-fated Audrey Mary and, a reflective moment bringing painful memories flooding to the fore, I shed bitter tears of regret as Nellie places her in the crook of my arm, pulling down the edge of the shawl and whispering in my ear as she peers in, but I don't need reminding because Audrey Mary's face is etched deep in memory.

By the time Harry responds to the urgent summons, issued by the beckoning hand of an anxious woman peering round the door of the Farfield Inn, all signs of recent birth have disappeared and an unusual calm has descended within the squat house on Thirza Street. Prioritising events, he had consumed three further pints in order to quench his insatiable thirst for Gilmour's ales and, the world's problems uppermost in his mind, had spent considerable time in serious discussion with other alcohol-motivated 'politicians' on the hump of Hillfoot Bridge. A howling blizzard driving him home, he stumbles over the back doorstep covered in a fine blanket of snow, a trail of slushy water tracking his progress into the living room. Clumsily throwing his saturated jacket over the clothes horse alongside Nellie's, he hooks his soggy cap on the opposite end-post. Staggering, he perilously crouches in front of the hearth, stirring dull coals in the fire grate and spreading ice cold hands before the waking blaze.

Footsteps descending the stairway, he hauls himself upright, fearing the worst when Nellie ambles into the room, face solemn, a stiff forefinger pointing in the direction of the bedroom above. Settling, heavily, on a chair by the table she stares at Harry, rubbing her chin thoughtfully, and, afraid some terrible tragedy had occurred, he momentarily sobers, his face suddenly a pale shade of grey. A dedicated non-believer, he nevertheless resorts to silent prayer in his desperation, but in a voice several decibels higher than usual, Nellie angrily rebukes him. Harry unwittingly mimics my father! Back stiff as a poker, head held high, nostrils flaring, a dark scowl creates thick horizontal ridges across his forehead, deep crevices between flashing eyes and, senses impaired, he struggles to translate furious thoughts into words. Taking swift advantage of his confusion Nellie ploughs on but, noting warning signs, she treads carefully. Not a drain of colour staining his cheek, Harry glares at Nellie and knowing she ventures on dangerous ground, she takes precautionary measures. Noisily scraping the chair from beneath her she waddles hurriedly across the room, retrieves her hat and coat and, pulling them on at speed, makes a swift exit through the kitchen. Clumsily dragging on boots standing just inside the back door, she wrenches it wide and heads swiftly for the safety of the back yard. Carefully negotiating a deep snowdrift beneath the kitchen window, she momentarily peers in, horrified at the sight of Harry making stumbling progress in her direction. Swiftly disappearing into the darkness of the passageway alongside, however, a resounding thud tells her the back door has taken the brunt of his anger.

Later going down to the Farfield, Harry has celebrations in mind and, following local tradition, he joins drinking partners in a crude ceremony involving the consumption of numerous pints of beer to 'wet' the baby's head in advance of a church service and prematurely naming her Carol, for obvious reasons. Suitably inebriated, a raucous bunch launch into a medley of Christmas songs in recognition of a long-ago birth. An act that is totally hypocritical since poverty and struggle has rendered many committed atheists.

The 'Peace in our Time' declaration, delivered by Chamberlain on his return from Germany, proves worthless and long-held fears realised, men and women are called to the aid of the country to prevent the predatory advance of the Hun. Some drafted into service, others urgently turning the wheels of industry, churning out a mountain of goods to feed the insatiable appetite of the war machine. Mills and factories back in full swing, Neepsend's heartbeat throbs again, cobbled streets ring with the clatter of clogged feet, smoking chimneys once more cast a dark veil. Routine returning to aimless lives, sense of purpose to meaningless days, cynicism becomes patriotism, dissatisfaction stoicism, as men and women rise to the defence of England. Call-up papers arriving on his door mat Harry joins the ranks of marching men, anti-establishment ideas temporarily shelved.

Carried on the wings of a brisk following wind, bad news tears around Neepsend. Swiftly passing from door to door it causes a furore along the way leaving many distressed people in its wake, because Nancy has unexpectedly died in prison. Striking yet another cruel blow, it finally arrives at my door, courtesy of an excited neighbour. Sidestepping the bearer, I race over the cobbled yard to the outside toilet urgently thrusting my head over the toilet pan, expelling the contents of my stomach. Slowly surrendering to a darkening whirlpool, I slump, in a crumpled heap, against the cold brick wall, but, cold light of day gradually emerging, stark reality brings a return of oppressive black moods, again snatching the meaning from life. Bearing alone the guilt and shame of a shady past, I hide from the world, venturing outdoors only when extremely necessary and, restless in their caged existence, bored toddlers vent their frustration in daily tantrums, while the new born screams with indignation at hours of neglect in the depths of the grubby bucket pram. Each night, lying awake re-living events and shedding pointless tears of despair, exhaustion saps every ounce of physical and mental strength, and, witnessing, with some concern, the growing neglect of home and family, neighbours rally while I urgently seek help at the recently opened South Yorkshire Lunatic Asylum's day centre.

Harry is feeling far from compassionate on arriving back in Sheffield. Razor-sharp creases run along Air Force blue trousers, rows of freshly polished gilt buttons and a winged badge attached to the front of an up-turned boat of a cap catch the glint of the sun. His weight has plummeted, his uniform hangs loose against his puny frame. Suitcase swinging from his fingers he turns into Thirza Street and, jaded, he appears far from enthusiastic at the prospect of returning home, his shoulders hunched, tired footsteps dragging along the cobblestones. Familiar chaotic sounds drifting from a grubby front window, he draws to a halt outside, seemingly reluctant to face old problems. Recent coughing bouts draining his energy, he rests his back against the brick wall, chest rasping as he gasps for air. Lurching forward, he presses a spread palm against each kneecap, violently coughing and spluttering in an attempt to force clogging mucus from his lungs. Face a pale shade of purple, lips a light blue hue he finally brings up a huge blood-stained globule angrily spitting it into the gutter. About to place his key in the lock he is visibly shaken at the sight confronting him from the top doorstep. Medicinally cushioned from reality eyes vacant and sunken, face sallow, body wasted, I am a shadow of my former self, and it's clear I have paid a high price for past actions. No mutual instinctive urge to reach beyond the barrier time and life have created, it's as if we are strangers and the chill silence bodes ill for a leave intended to help my mental suffering and repair the broken home.

In quick succession, blow after blow rains down and news of yet another pregnancy, coinciding with the delivery of an urgent telegram leaves me clinging by a flimsy thread to the real world because, a victim of tuberculosis, Harry has been urgently transferred from a military medical establishment to the nearby dreaded Winter Street Hospital in Sheffield. A huge red-brick building, often proving the final resting place for those regularly inhaling industry's potent poisonous cocktail, its name carries fearful local connotations. Barely able to negotiate the flight of steps leading to the entrance, most climb slowly, regularly pausing to gulp in desperately needed air. Urgently transported by ambulance, others entering its doors are gravely ill, faces blue and purple from lack of oxygen and many leave in wooden boxes. In this atmosphere of ill-foreboding, Harry fights for life.

On a clear night in December 1940 a bright moon lights the winding route of the Don, guiding German aircraft to Neepsend. Shrill, doom-laden sirens scream out a warning, frantic people scuttle for the safety of air raid shelters as the ominous drone of approaching enemy aircraft fills the skies. Some place their faith in the Almighty, desperately praying as the shrill whistle of hurtling bombs draw near, but even the all-powerful is incapable of holding back the barrage and, thunderous explosions rocking the ground, the smell of fear permeates dark hideaways. In the ensuing silence bewildered people stare out at scenes of desolation. Amidst palls of black smoke, flames of red and orange shoot through factory roofs, burning tramcars tip into massive craters blown into cobbled roads, tiny houses disintegrate in the wake of the bombardment. During two days of frenzied attack, Neepsend is blitzed and at the final 'all clear' people gaze in horror at the scenes of destruction. Ghostly apparitions, mere shells of houses stand exposed to inclement weather and, collapsed, others form piles of rubble, but amongst the desolation some stand firm. Bewildered people wander amongst the carnage, some clawing at the earth with bare hands in search of missing friends or relatives possibly buried beneath, others stand dazed, unable to comprehend the horror of it all. A cacophony of human suffering, frantic screams ring across the smoke-filled air, clanging of bells and throaty sirens herald the approach of fire engines and ambulances urgently racing to the rescue. Bewildered, bedraggled and confused I wander amongst the ruins of our tiny house on Thirza Street and a trio of traumatised boys clinging to my coat tails, tiny new born screaming and writhing in the bucket pram, we finally join a gathering throng making their way to the nearest rest centre.

CHAPTER NINE
SHORT IDYLLIC DAYS

Winter is loosening its grip now, but in its final throes gently falling snow leaves a fine coating of white upon a sprawling landscape, and, spring around the corner, a bevy of flapping wings fill the air: starlings, house sparrows, crows and blackbirds brave its dying days. What contrast this to the stinking, dense fog of Neepsend, its streets struggling for daylight this time of year. How peaceful the natural world after its constant deafening din, alien the sweet smell of fresh air compared to its poisonous environment.

Standing awhile, Harry and I breathe in the wonder of it all. Though icy winds blow, unhindered, across the vast open expanse, frozen earth crunches beneath our feet and a snowy cap perches on every sloping roof top. We have arrived in paradise. Sadly, lying stark against lightly falling snow, a distant, dark barrage balloon sends out an ominous reminder of continuing hostilities and possible enemy attack as we tread a rough track to our new home on the fledgling Parson Cross estate. A phoenix rising from the ashes: new council houses, with gardens back and front, begin replacing the slums of yesteryear, lifting people from industry's dark shadows into better climes. Just within the border of the West Riding of Yorkshire the unfinished stretch of Fulmere Road has been dug out of open countryside and, exposed to raw elements, red brick houses bear the brunt of winter's last fling.

Despite plummeting temperatures, Harry and I stand watching Michael stumbling across the snowy waste, attempting to catch elusive snowflakes in cupped hands, Steven struggling to form a snowball from a handful of soft snow, eventually sending it loosely scattering into space. Loitering at a distance, Peter keeps watch over our last born, clumsily attempting first steps, sense of responsibility too soon taking away his childhood. An ailing couple, Harry and I struggle with the remainder of the journey and, bringing us both to a halt, Harry stands, mouth gaping, desperately sucking in air, and my eyes dulled by medication, troubled gaze fixed on the earth, progress is painfully slow over the final stretch.

From front windows, newly installed neighbours watch our laboured approach, no doubt immediately recognising my medically induced, unnatural gait, stiffness and blank expression, my bulging waistline telling them there will soon be another addition to our swiftly expanding family.

The house verges on palatial. Government funding affording us an oak bedroom suite and matching double bed for the front bedroom, double bed for each at the back. A bulky brown Rexine suite, oak dining table and chairs with matching sideboard, grace the living room and it's a far cry from the cramped, damp conditions on Thirza Street. A large cast iron range, set in the chimney breast, serves many purposes and when a fire burns in the grate it sends heat along two flues, one feeding the oven the other a back-boiler, heating water in the cistern above. Tin bath, single cold water tap, claustrophobic living and a pitiful past buried beneath the ruins of Thirza Street we are immediately at ease and at home. No longer hemmed in by dark factories, overlooked by row after row of cramped terraces, surrounded by concrete, brick and stone or choked by industrial smog, Utopia stretches for miles outside our front and back windows.

Medically discharged from the Air Force, Harry begins his recuperation in the most beneficial surroundings, nature's healing powers freely at hand and, though financially poor, we are rich beyond belief in this country idyll. Setting the children free I gradually learn to relax, their romping forms always running freely in the fields opposite, voices ringing across the sprawling back garden. Harry always on hand, black clouds of depression slowly begin to disperse, and each day carrying me further along the road to recovery, scars of the past begin to heal. Sense of pride in home and family returning, my old self emerges with each passing day. Each week, black-leading the range and fender, polishing furniture to a brilliant sheen, I toil over wash tub, rubbing board and mangle, boiling 'whites' in the copper boiler alongside the kitchen sink. A long-lost sense of pride returning, I display the results of my efforts along a washing line strung almost the full length of the back garden, on wet days draping them over a clothes horse in front of the fire and it's all a labour of love.

My confident comings and goings, balm to Harry's soul, he perches on the back step, face spread in a contented smile as he recuperates in the glorious fresh air. Elbows propped on his knees, chin resting in cupped hands, birdsong in the air, washing flapping in the breeze, instil an unfamiliar feeling of perfect peace and, inspired, he whistles a lilting tune of his own composition. Applying dubious cobbling skills, he squats on his haunches in the back porch, worn shoes scattered around him, a row of half-inch five-eighths nails gripped in clenched teeth and, pressing each shoe in turn on the hobbing foot, he cuts leather to shape with an old boy scout knife, nailing it in place and carefully trimming the excess. Convinced his skills rival those of a professional cobbler, he flatly refuses to believe the evidence of his own eyes or disgruntled cries on return to their owners, when some tended to rock instead of standing flat on the ground.

Singing a tremulous version of 'Mary Ellen at the Church Turned Up,' he occasionally potters around rough plots at the back and front of the house, keenly planning their further use and, propped in the bucket pram on the backyard, Carol looks out onto the world from beneath the half-haloed brim of a straw bonnet, unaware of its dangers. Snowdrops leading the way, spring arrives in indecisive mood and, despite an occasional late wintry shower arriving on blustery winds, rays of bright sunshine finally break through winter's chill. Emerging from seasonal hibernation, crocuses push flimsy heads through the earth, birds flit overhead, filling the air with birdsong – a skylark's distinctive whistle dominating the chorus as it plummets to its nest in the ground. Monotonously humming, bees harvest pollen from the heads of wide-eyed moonpennies, and blood-red poppies sway en masse, amongst the grass in the fields outside our front window stretching way into the distance. Cabbage White and Red Admiral butterflies erratically flit from petal to delicate petal and, on the horizon, tiny farm cottages nestle amongst chequered fields of brown, green and yellow. Dark, dry-stone walls form irregular boundaries, marking out the countryside. Half their bodies above ground, Italian and German prisoners-of-war toil in deep trenches, laying the foundations for expansion, in broken English calling out a friendly greeting as people pass by. Shirt sleeves rolled above their elbows, picks and shovels temporarily at rest, some relax in the sunshine, skilfully fashioning clay pipes for local children from the clay beneath their feet.

Harry benefits greatly from a daily dose of wonderful vinous air and spring gradually giving way to summer, he plans a voyage of discovery. A ray of sunlight slanting through a gap in the curtains at the bedroom window, he hurries out of bed, throwing them wide and inviting in a glorious summer sun. He peers across the open expanse opposite, absorbing the wonderful view. Sitting high over still fields, the huge yellow sun sets alight every droplet of morning dew settled on the grass and in the distance two cart horses move, in unison, laboriously hauling a plough over a half-furrowed field, heads simultaneously nodding towards the earth. Following close behind, a farmer treads tilled earth, sheepdog running at his heels. Birds serenade from nearby treetops and, inspired, he hurries down, keen to teach his own the wonders of nature he had only read about in books.

Beneath a cloudless sky, we forge an erratic path through a mass of wild flowers, gradually leaving behind the lone stretch of houses. Perched upon Harry's forearm, Carol silently absorbs the wonders of the world around, huge brown eyes tracking the movement of birds on the wing, occasional butterfly in flight. Carelessly kicking up flowers, Peter and Steven race in giddy circles, voices echoing across the silence as they chase each other into the distance. Vainly attempting to share their enjoyment, Michael stumbles at a distance, face sullen.

Climbing over wooden stiles we cross from furrowed to grassy field eventually chancing across the quaint old village of Ecclesfield and, coming to rest outside the centuries old St. Mary's church standing on a raised pedestal of land at its centre. Struggling to recall scant architectural knowledge, gleaned during school days, Harry studies lines and curves of the imposing building, wavering between Saxon and Norman and finally leaving the subject alone. Church bells sombrely tolling the hour, he leads us past the open doors of the Black Bull public house opposite and into the nearby village square. The White Bear, the Tankard, the Griffin Inn, huddling in close proximity. Harry finally brings us to rest on wooden forms beneath the window of the Griffin Inn with the words GILMOUR'S ALES etched into a half-frosted pane. Soon, carrying a tin tray bearing a glass of sweet sherry, pint of ale and bottles of orange, straws protruding, Harry settles alongside us and, in a state of quiet contentment, we quench thirsts generated by stifling heat.

Remnants from a bygone age, wooden stocks stand in the centre of the village square, prompting a barrage of questions from inquisitive boys and, imagination fired, Harry becomes embroiled in a wildly exaggerated tale. Conjuring a fictitious character from the depths, he paints a graphic picture of a frantic little man, clamped by arms and legs, being pelted with rotten fruit by screaming assailants. Spellbound and chuckling, the boys swallow his tale hook, line and sinker and, embellishing historical fact, Harry goes further, telling of how the poor man had developed an all-over rash and had to walk the streets of Ecclesfield swathed, from head to foot, in bandages as if an Egyptian mummy. How some wags, turning out of the Black Bull the worse for wear, had taken out drink-induced devilment on him, firmly gripping the end of the bandage and spinning him until, released, he careered like a spinning top along Church Street, only the timely intervention of a lamp standard slowing his momentum and preventing him landing in a pile of steamy droppings left by a passing horse pulling a cart.

Encouraged by hysterical laughter Harry's enthusiasm grows and, a consummate spinner of yarns, he ventures on a further tale of yet another imaginary victim being dragged to the nearby fishing pond and made to sit on a ducking stool attached to the end of a platform extended over the water. Throughout the narration, repeatedly shaking his head and gulping like a grounded fish, he demonstrates how the woman had gasped for air on being repeatedly plunged into the murk below, tears of laughter streaming down the boy's faces on hearing she emerged from the final ducking with a large trout flapping between her teeth. Explaining that the woman was a witch, he terrified Michael.

Having been regaled with stories of witches and their frightening exploits throughout childhood, he screams fit to wake the dead in the nearby churchyard and, serving a penance, Harry is forced to carry him shoulder high along a rugged path skirting a nearby cornfield. Sharing his punishment, I struggle through increasing heat, a tetchy Carol struggling in my arms, but we are both distracted when two large hares spring from amidst the corn, quickly disappearing into a hillock on the other side. Euphoria carrying us through the searing heat of mid-afternoon, we seek relief beneath a thick canopy of trees in Grenoside Woods.

Forever inventive, Steven searches the ground, eventually selecting a suitable fallen branch, stripping it of leaves and shadow-fencing in a mock battle with an imaginary foe. Tentatively feeling for safe footholds amongst spreading branches, Peter shins to dizzy heights settling in the fork of an old oak and, peering through thick foliage across a vast wooded expanse, he tastes complete solitude for the first time in his life. Falling across the woodland floor, dark shadows revive frightening memories and vividly imagining witches flying overhead on broomsticks, black cloaks wafting in the wind, pointed hats accentuating long noses, voices chanting as they come to rest around a blazing camp fire, Michael hovers close to Harry. Strangely, Harry's crafty promise of a possible sighting of a lion or tiger distracts and, watching him tiptoe through thick undergrowth, eyes flitting in his quest, we all laugh at his eager anticipation. Showing no sign of fear, he carefully parts the undergrowth, ironically searching for dangerous animals portrayed in children's books as lovable, cuddly pets with doleful eyes and a tendency to befriend humans. Nearby rustling brings him to a sudden halt and, suspecting a magical emergence, he waits, mouth gaping, but only a bushy-tailed squirrel scampers by, scurrying up the trunk of a giant elm on its way to a ragged home in the fork of spreading branches.

Hoisting themselves on the top of a 5-bar gate on the return journey, legs dangling, Peter and Steven gaze across surrounding landscape, watching horses romp, kick up their heels and whinny with excitement at heady freedom in a grassy paddock bounded by hawthorn bushes. Leaning against a supporting post, Michael wrestles with flickering eyelids and, hoisting him upward, Harry settles him on his forearm, head hanging loosely over his shoulder, eyes closing. In the crook of my arm, Carol sleeps peacefully and, sidling close, Harry and I linger awhile silently absorbing the peace of nature's garden.

Stumbling across an old farm on the homeward journey we lean over a weathered stone wall, watching chickens peck at a scattering of seed or occasional earthworm foolishly rearing its head above the soil and, a shrill 'cock-a-doodle-do' piercing the countryside, a lone cockerel treads an erratic path across slushy ground. Startling us all, a nearby strutting goose careers in pursuit of a barking sheepdog, wings flapping wildly and, stored beneath the canopy of an open barn, steaming heaps of rotting manure send out a repugnant smell. Nipping noses between index finger and thumb, we hurry by in a vain bid to escape its wafting. As if to compensate, a warm breeze soon carries the sweet scent of hawthorn as we cross a roughly-constructed wooden style into a field bounded by rich, green bushes and, picking up the sound of running water, Peter and Steven eagerly trace its source to a crystal-clear spring tumbling from a dry-stone wall; drinking, copiously from cupped hands soothes throats, parched from walking long hours in the sun.

Sliding down a grassy incline, tentatively balancing on huge boulders forming stepping stones across a meandering stream, they run, breathlessly, up the grassy slope opposite, coming to a halt at the sight of grazing cattle inquisitively lifting huge heads to peer from the corner of huge, hooded eyes, rich green grass, newly hauled from the earth, dangling either side of thick lips. Ears twitching, tails swishing in a bid to deter flies they chew slowly, eyes fixed on the warily approaching pair and, despite their urgent beckoning, both Harry and I are otherwise engaged.

A snoozing Michael precariously balanced on his forearm, Harry crouches by the stream picking fresh watercress for tea and, cradled in my lap in the long grass, Carol suckles contentedly, but, despite Harry's reassurance that his grasp of animal language and confident calling of 'Coosh lass' will keep the curious animals at bay, I am equally dubious when forced to pass between them. Courage finally failing, Peter and Steven take flight, racing up a small flight of steps and laughing at my nervous weaving amongst tetchy cattle, from the safety of Wheel Lane. Casually strolling at a distance, Harry laughs at my unnecessary fear.

On the final leg of the journey, Harry guides us along a narrow path running through a small wooded copse and, echoing through space, the frantic whinny of a nearby horse rudely rouses Michael from his slumber. Indignant screams filling the air, Harry reacts instinctively. Lowering him to the ground he cautiously reaches into a gorse bush tentatively parting prickly branches to reveal a hollowed nest skilfully woven from fine grass and lined with feathers. Rising on tiptoe, Peter and Steven peer in enthralled at the sight of a clutch of speckled eggs nestling in the darkness. More a man of the soil than the city Harry reaches in and, completely at one with nature, he gently draws one into the light cupping it in the palm of his hand in front of wide-eyed Michael. Drawing on knowledge gleaned from his school days he explains that a young linnet is forming inside and that, feeding on flaxseed, it will later fill the warm spring air with charming song. Absorbing his every word the boys gather around, eyes wide with admiration. Mesmerised, they watch his every move as he carefully replaces the egg and pulls spread branches back in place to protect the young from possible predators. Emanating from the top of a nearby bush tuneful twittering warns that the mother bird is keeping a wary eye on proceedings.

Energy flagging, a crocodile line finally makes its ragged journey home. A sleeping Carol cradled in his arms, Harry leads the way, two weary boys drag their heels close behind and bringing up the rear I gradually encourage a dawdling Michael over the final steps. A weary path forged, we bring back souvenirs. An abundance of wild flowers lay over Peter's arm, daisy chains hang around Carol and Michael's neck and drifting from Steven's shoes, the unpleasant stench of cow dung serves as a reminder of a clumsy dash to safety across the cow field.

At the end of a wonderful, exhilarating day we gather around the dining table beneath the front window, recalling its adventures over an evening meal, a carefully-arranged display of flowers, springing from a glass jug at the centre of the table, keeping rich memories alive. At last, tucking contented children into bed, I flop, exhausted and happy, into an armchair by the hearth, tired legs resting on the fender, Verdi's Rigolleto escaping into the night through the open window. Perched on the back step, Harry packs Bruno tobacco deep into the bowl of his pipe puffing, thoughtfully, on its stem and releasing thin trails of smoke into gathering greyness as the sun goes down.

Eventually strong enough to till rough earth, Harry creates vegetable patches along the back garden, plants raspberry canes and rhubarb crowns alongside a red brick air raid shelter at the bottom, a young blackberry bush beneath the kitchen window. Having carefully studied boundary walls criss-crossing the countryside on our travels, he applies natural artistic skills, building a curving dry-stone wall around the perimeter a short distance away from a distinctive, sapling yellow privet edge neatly trimmed to a height conducive to easy maintenance. Filling the empty space behind with soil, he plants raised beds of wallflowers, iris, golden rod and red-hot pokers, sparing no effort on building a raised circular stone wall as a centrepiece. Similarly filling it with soil, he randomly scatters seeds to create a riot of colour and to scent the air with delicate perfumes as seasons permit. Fastidiously tending his work of art, he instantly plucks out weeds daring to raise their heads above the soil and, trilling like a songbird, I perform endless household tasks purely for the pleasure and satisfaction of it all.

Fulmere Road becomes home to a rich mix of people from the war-torn slums of Sheffield, some keen to leave behind the filth and grime of industrial areas and the stigma of living in their shadows, others mourning the loss of familiar faces and places, keeping them warm during years of poverty and the terrible experience of war, but, very soon, a community begins to develop and each day brings a bright new dawn. Almost as soon as Carol vacates the bucket pram a new born takes her place and, in line with local tradition, the infant crosses no other threshold until after the day of her christening.

Harry's church a public house, prayer book a pint glass, he argues against attending on a point of principle but, after much heated discussion, agreeing to join me on the understanding that we part company at the end of the service. Snuggled inside a borrowed silk christening gown and crocheted shawl our latest first sees Fulmere Road through a fine lace veil and, although a pale pink sun sits high in the sky, a sprinkling of raindrops cut through a fine haze. A mere April shower, it quickly ceases, leaving the air smelling of damp earth but, in the distance a bank of ominous black cloud climbs over the horizon, quickly forming a canopy overhead and plunging the streets into darkness as we hurry towards the church of St. Cecilia.

Surrounded by a semi-circle of newly-built council houses the imposing stone church appears ill-placed in the cramped space but, a high church rooted in strong traditions, it draws in the dedicated. Twin stone crosses rise from one end of a pitched roof, a single square turret the other. Latin mass, ceremonial robes, breaking of bread and drinking of wine are the order of the day. A familiar figure in the neighbourhood, Father Mahoney regularly walks his 'patch,' black frock coat brushing his ankles. Black three-cornered hat pressed on his greying hair, he acquaints himself with newcomers to the gradually expanding neighbourhood. As a shepherd watching over his sheep he spreads his biblical message in the newly-built Parson Cross Hotel, chatting to local people over glass-strewn tables and, though partial to a glass or two of whisky himself, makes believe his visits are purely pastoral and for the purpose of converting those considered to have fallen by the wayside. In the piety of the stone church he assumes the dignity of a man of Christ.

Contemplative worshippers already filter from the arched doorway, shaking hands with the vicar and thanking him for their deliverance on their departure, as we arrive. Despite cynicism and their rejection of the church as an institution, a small group of non-worshippers congregate in the pouring rain, umbrellas raised overhead, new babies cradled in their arms. Old wives' tales and early religious experiences leaving an impression sufficient to fear the Lord, they wait to take out insurance in the hope of protecting offspring against the wrath of God and hell and damnation believed to await heathens on the other side.

In full traditional garb, a prayer book clasped against his chest beneath crossed palms, Father Mahoney inspires a quiet reverence, beckoning the crocodile procession into the arched porch, a raised hand tracing a cross on the air as he leads them into the House of God. Seated at a huge organ between choir stalls the organist teases out a chord and, accompanied by the strains of 'Jesu Lover of my Soul,' the solemn procession passes between rows of wooden pews, eyes fixed on the altar ahead. Walking slowly alongside, a lay member of the church swings an incense burner filling the air with a pungent smell invoking a sense of serenity and spiritual peace.

Marble robe stretching from head to flimsy sandals, crown of thorns pressed on long tresses, Christ looks down from a marble plinth arms outstretched, open palms beckoning and, under his watchful gaze, a reverential group gather around a stone font. Symbolic of their role as substitute parents, godparents, one by one, pass new offspring into the waiting arms of Father Mahoney and, chanting a solemn blessing, he dips his fingers into the stone font tracing a damp cross across each tiny forehead and welcoming them into the House of God. Witnessing the occasion Archangel Gabriel looks down from a huge, arched stained glass window high above the altar golden, halo hovering, hands lightly resting upon the tiny shoulders of young kneeling children. Cut in brilliant hues, Matthew, Mark, Luke and John peer from another stained-glass window at the opposite end of the church.

Finally stepping into the greyness of late morning, I lift the lace veil from Celia's face, safe in the knowledge that, having paid her premiums in full, she is now a bona fide member of the Lord's flock. Nevertheless, even on closing the doors behind us, I know Father Mahoney is in no doubt that he will only ever see us on his doorstep again in times of need.

War still raging, threat of attack ever present, it is a time of fear and austerity but for now the world is our oyster, each season offering simple pleasures fostering a state of heady contentment. Spring rains pave the way for fresh carpets of flowers outside our window, summer sends sultry breezes, early autumn nature's bounties and over long, lazy days we walk for miles; sometimes collecting blackberries from bushes crawling over the slope of Back Edge or bilberries from bushy mounds roaming over open moorland. Haunting scream of a curlew, whistle of grouse or unseen meadow pipit, strange cry of a pheasant breaks the eerie silence but the shrill, desperate scream of a frantic young animal, caught in the grip of a foraging stoat, cry of a predatory sparrow hawk swooping to earth in a swift kill reminds of nature's dark side. Strong winds and driving rain bringing sweet chestnuts to earth, Peter and Steven brave plummeting temperatures, clambering up giant trees and foraging amongst a carpet of fallen leaves in Grenoside Woods. Their pockets bulging on their way home in readiness for bonfire night, which, it being wartime, is carried out indoors: the only 'bonfire' in the firegrate, a few iron filings scattered on the flames the 'fireworks.'

Winter returning, heavy frost again blankets the earth, breath freezes on the air, bitter winds whisk heavy snowfalls into a frenzy, icy draughts blow a gale through the house but, despite freezing temperatures and scant cobbles burning in the fire grate, the closeness of family keeps us warm. Retiring indoors, Harry and I scrape ice from the front window, peering over the vast open expanse of white opposite, watching excited children at play. A distant, heavily-laden, sky merges with a landscape, now nature's natural playground and, enthralled by boundless freedom, some chase one another into the distance leaving a zig-zag trail in their wake. Others haul one another over undulating ground on make-shift sledges, fling snowballs across the freezing air screaming with delight at stunned expressions of unsuspecting victims. Pebble eyes vacantly staring into space, snowmen, with carrot noses and twig lips, magically rise from the earth and, pleasures manifold, freezing conditions are no deterrent to children lacking warm winter clothing, playing until light fades, extremities turn blue and chilblains set in.

Oh! That I could forever rest in those short idyllic days! Yet the scene already changing, I know the cruel future still beckons! In my spiritual state, I squeeze tight my eyes in a desperate bid to prevent its re-telling but instinctively I know there is no escape!

CHAPTER TEN
BACK TO SQUARE ONE

Heady, halcyon days change us all, and, pale haunted face giving way to a more youthful bloom, emaciated body to a more feminine shape, the old Alice is back and each day is filled with domestic activity and childish laughter. No longer gaunt with sickly pallor, Harry has benefitted from long hours in the open air, his cheeks pink, eyes bright, body less wasted and, a troubled past firmly behind us, a more secure future beckons when he finally finds work as a trainee window-frame maker with a firm at the other end of town.

Sadly, instead of bringing prosperity into our lives, employment reminds Harry there is a life beyond the four walls of home and freedoms of the past beckon. Workplace injustice rekindling political interest, he regularly links up with long-lost friends in old watering holes as in days gone by, immersing himself in Union affairs, challenging authority and generally fighting 'the cause'. Ironically, whilst seeking to defend the rights of others he neglects those of his own and, travelling in masculine circles, natural chauvinistic tendencies come to the fore. Asserting his right to privacy he weekly shreds evidence of his earnings, flushing it down the toilet pan and handing over a pittance for upkeep of home and family. His right to independence, flitting, free of encumbrance, in and out of the family home at will. One minute a weary workman returning from work in greasy bib-and-brace overalls for a quick meal and wash, the next a dapper figure in sports jacket and trousers, dashing out of the door leaving behind a whiff of Sunlight soap and all family responsibility.

Viewing my domestic role as a feminine calling and less important than his own, he takes for granted my seven days a week unbroken commitment, but family and home are the very oxygen of my existence. Sighting an interesting set of old encyclopaedias in a second-hand shop on Langsett Road, I secretly lay it away, long sacrifice paying off when the huge tomes rest in an old tin trunk in the back bedroom. On dismal days, when rain drizzles down the windows and black clouds imprison restless boys indoors, I am rewarded manifold. Naturally bright, they are held, rapt, for hours thumbing through endless pages, filling their heads with knowledge, beginnings of the world, structure and strata of the earth, planets, Greek philosophers and a plethora of subjects clearly explained and graphically illustrated, and, when Peter is amongst the very few to gain a scholarship to the prestigious Ecclesfield Grammar school, I swell with pride and hope for his future. His miserable past, a fading memory, mine finally laid to rest, I find inner peace at last. Climbing into bed at night, I sleep the deep sleep off the contented, conscience finally salved but, lost to the world until morning, fail to notice staggering footsteps finding their way home increasingly late at night or dark storm clouds gathering.

The heady fragrance of Ashes of Violets begins to permeate the hallway at Fulmere Road, and, as it drifts aromatic from the wash tub, it does no more than revive fleeting memories of long-ago carefree days when personal care had been my main consideration, pride paramount. But the moments are swept away in hectic domestic routine. Regularly returning, they begin sowing ugly seeds of doubt and, mentally running over recent weeks I realise that, under my very nose, Harry has changed. Fading interest in family life, irate complaints about the tiniest speck of dirt on freshly laundered shirts, irritation at every turn as if troubled, he has been distant. Every single, insignificant detail amounting to a sinister, significant whole, things appear to point to one irrefutable fact. A molehill gradually rising to the terrifying heights of a mountain sends me hurtling towards a precipice, a familiar black hole opening up before me but, at the very peak of endurance, I fall to earth with a bump. Too terrified to believe the worst, I chastise myself for my stupidity and, re-winding events, view things from a different perspective, certain Harry is incapable of disloyalty, that his new-found confidence and pride is a product of renewed independence and the influence of others at work, feminine perfume on his clothing a result of some careless brush alongside a female on a crowded tram.

When it begins wafting from his person with frightening regularity, I am desperately afraid. Confrontation my natural instinct, I, nevertheless, manage to curb a burning desire to rant, rave and force him into a corner, instead settling on a plan to either prove his innocence or catch him red-handed. Every day sets a new challenge and with the keenness of a tracker dog routinely sniffing every inch of his jacket in the hallway, I fervently pray I am barking up the wrong tree! Only the flimsiest traces of Ashes of Violets remaining, I castigate myself for lack of trust and, fears gradually allayed, am about to abort my probing when a tell-tale lipstick stain stops me dead in my tracks. Legs buckling, I examine the jacket lapel more closely and, jury out, the indisputable outline of well-shaped lips presents proof I so desperately wanted to avoid.

Blind panic drives me to vengeful thoughts. Thinking skewed, an irrational, vindictive urge impels me to immediately catch the tram and confront him at work, demanding the name of his floozy and deliberately humiliating him in front of workmates. Instead, an overwhelming wave of conflicting senses drive me, on leaden feet, into the bathroom and body trembling, head hung over the toilet bowl I purge my anguish. Stumbling into the living room, I carelessly throw back the curtains but though a bright shaft of sunlight bursts through a black cloud descends. Mind fragile, all I want to do is to wallow in the horror of my find and, instead of the customary light-hearted banter, harsh words hasten the boys' departure to school. In the bedroom above, neglected children weep, wail and whimper but, pre-occupied, I slump into the arm chair by the hearth, hair and clothing dishevelled.

On the boys' return from school, they make an uncertain entrance and it is clear the day has passed me by because nothing has changed from the morning, save a bewildered Carol who kneels alongside me in her nightclothes, eyes closed, head resting in my lap, tiny body heaving from hours of sobbing. Hysterical cries drift from the back bedroom, dirty crockery clutters the table and a heavy chill hangs in the air because yesterday's ashes still lay cold in the grate. Unable to rouse me from my stupor, the boys automatically create order from chaos, carrying distressed siblings downstairs, washing, feeding, changing each one before tucking them into bed at the end of a day that, for them, had never started. Painful memories revived, the boys retire to their own beds, fearful the dreadful past has returned to haunt.

Cutting sharply through the silence, the shrill yapping of a neighbour's terrier dog prompts me into sudden wakefulness, shocking me from my bemused state and leaving me confused as to how the night has returned without my knowledge. Curtains still wide apart, a brilliant yellow moon sends a beam of light cutting through the blackness of the room and a dark shadow bending against the back wall, I lean forward, checking the time on the mantel clock. Five minutes past midnight. Stumbling footsteps making unsteady progress along the street outside set my senses racing and vivid memories come flooding back. Overcome with sadistic pleasure at the thought of imminent revenge, I track each one and, as Harry carefully turns the backdoor knob, preparing for silent entry, wrench it from his grasp. A dishevelled figure lunging out of the darkness, I grip him by the lapels of his jacket clumsily hauling him over the threshold and in the flurry, the unmistakable aroma wafts beneath my nose. Unleashing weeks of frustration, I launch a violent attack, screaming accusations with every blow. Locked in a frenzied embrace we stumble around the kitchen and, scurrying footsteps lost in the foray, three startled faces appear around the stair's door. Anxious glances flitting up and down my dishevelled state and wild expression, I recoil in horror and, young footsteps immediately retreating up the stairway, I already know my past is working against me. Knowing that testing parental loyalty will only add to their burden, I desperately battle against the urge to call them back and explain, but silence leaving me with no defence, I slouch, defeated, against the kitchen wall.

Overnight, I toss and turn, mentally running over events and struggling to come to terms with the horror of it all and, yesterday an unbearable memory, tomorrow holding no promise, morning finds me in a morose state. The world around dull and uninviting. I meekly respond to Harry's impatient prompting and, reluctant to face the day, shuffle slowly out of bed, but, dressing carelessly, my blank expression sends prior warning that domesticity again beckons.

A dark menacing sprawl against a heavy sky, the South Yorkshire Lunatic Asylum beckons and, feet dragging, arm loosely linked in Harry's, I watch the ground disappearing beneath my feet as we tread the long, winding pathway to its huge wooden doors. Flanked by uniformed members of staff, an air of complete misery travels with me along stark corridors, my shuffling gait mingling with their more confident tread.

Minds and bodies in the paralysis of powerful drugs, inmates shuffle idly by in their daily boredom, movements wooden. Some lean against white-washed walls, silently watching our progress through vacant eyes. Once flexible faces fixed in strange grins and totally at ease in each other's company, two men stroll casually by, arms linked. Tall and wiry, an over-sized head set on narrow shoulders, one looks down on his stunted, bow-legged, companion nudging him with a bony elbow and nodding in my direction. Teeth and fingernails stained from eating her own faeces, a wizened old lady shuffles from a side ward, head uncontrollably shaking as she treads an unsteady path a short distance behind. A tall, middle-aged man with crude 'basin' haircut frighteningly stands in our way, tongue lolling, toothless grin contorting his features. Hands thrust deep into baggy trouser pockets, elastic braces stretched to full capacity, his turn-ups hang over his shoes and dignity is only marginally preserved. Stretching out a bony hand in my direction he lunges forward begging for a cigarette in monosyllabic tone but, mercifully, I miss the horror of it all. Mentally exhausted, I inhabit a world of my own far away from the madness inside and outside the asylum.

Gentle prompting of asylum staff gradually extracting problems, I pour out my anguish, but garbled claims of Harry's unfaithfulness prompt only sympathetic nods, and patronising smiles tell me there is an element of disbelief. Terrified my past might determine my future, I panic and, desperate sobs punctuating frantic outpourings, it seems my inability to calmly explain is fuelling suspicions of delusion. Consigned to a side ward, I wile away the time amongst other tranquillised females, constantly pacing in a state of utter despair and helplessness and, eventually withdrawing from the world, sit alone in quiet corners dwelling on thoughts of home, but the days are long and Fulmere Road seems so far away now.

Inside those awful walls a community has developed, its grapevine filtering messages, like wildfire, to every member and, when dreaded news of imminent shock treatment is mysteriously leaked, anxious inmates spread the word in hushed tones and a curtain of fear descends. Having suffered its horrors, victims live in fear of more, others, yet to succumb, survive each day in a state of abject terror fuelled by terrifyingly graphic descriptions. Existing in self-imposed isolation, how was I to know what was waiting in the wings?

Escorted, dull and lifeless, to a clinical white-walled room I innocently lie on the starched white sheet, every voice and footfall echoing as white-coated staff flit around, eventually arriving alongside and tinkering with a piece of menacing-looking equipment. Instinctively recoiling from their grasp on their approach, I frantically struggle but, manfully pinned to the bed, I am as an animal snared. Eyes wide, I watch proceedings, terrified at every sinister move. As one attaches electrodes at various angles across my scalp, another clamps my tongue to prevent choking, foiling my ability to remind them I am human. Frantically searching their faces for signs of humility, disturbed by their cold eyes and clinical approach, I can see long experience has hardened them to the task and humility been destroyed by its familiarity.

Their power greater than mine I have no choice but to surrender and, a switch thrown, surges of electricity instantly race to source. Thrust into a nightmare scenario, every fibre of my being springs to life and, nerves twitching, muscles contracting and expanding with every current, I dramatically jerk and heave, startled eyes silently pleading for mercy. Their inhuman treatment finally ceased, I lie still and deathly pale in the sudden calm, sunken eyes gaping, skin clammy, every drop of energy spent.

Self-imposed isolation only invites more, but repeat sessions gradually strip away my personality until I present to the world the same shocked persona as other inmates subjected to the same soul-destroying ordeal. Eyes blank, lines of suffering deeply etched, it's clear I have suffered damage and, when Harry finally meets me in reception he takes home a different person. Openly displaying traits of having been subjected to treatment in a mental institution, I walk slowly alongside him down the tree-lined driveway and though shafts of bright sunlight cut through still branches, their light fails to penetrate my strange world.

Spirit crushed I smell no floral perfumes on the breeze, see no colour in plants and flowers along its borders and, though birds flit overhead, I hear no birdsong because I have been stripped of senses giving vitality and meaning to life. A part of my soul stolen within those cruel walls, the outside world is daunting because there is no place for those becoming strange products of the asylum, its barred windows screaming of dangerous inmates. Readily identifiable, I am the butt of cruel attention and, people pointing and staring as we pass by, I huddle close to Harry, a lighted cigarette bearing witness to my recently adopted habit.

News of yet another pregnancy further rocks my world and suspicion continuing to haunt me daily, I teeter close to the edge. Craft and guile my main means of survival in the asylum, amongst others turned to petty thieves through lack of personal possessions, the art of cunning serves me well and my secret daily vigil continues on Harry's return to work. Incapable of fully picking up the threads of my old life, the house is run in haphazard fashion and body gradually swelling to gigantic proportions, life is a struggle throughout the closing months of pregnancy. Sapping remaining energy, the birth finally reduces me to human wreckage and, delivering my youngest to the gates of Rawsons Infant School in Ecclesfield, teachers are extremely alarmed at the pitiful sight trundling towards them. Angela, the newly born, restlessly whimpers beneath grubby blankets in the depth of the shabby bucket pram. Underweight and dishevelled, Carol runs in advance into the playground but Celia huddles close, dress ragged at the hemline, socks badly discoloured, sandals down-at-heel and she looks forlorn and desperately afraid when handed over.

Regarding State intervention as an attack on his masculinity, insult to his intelligence and nothing short of patronage, Harry resists offers of help but, inevitably, a smartly-dressed district nurse arrives on a bicycle, leather Gladstone bag secured to a small rack behind the saddle. In calf-length black coat, matching stockings and felt hat she calls weekly, tending Angela, bathing my two older girls and restoring matted hair to health but, mentally and physically weak, I lack motivation and the house is falling into a dreadful state.

In the belief that fresh air and regular exercise might help heal my broken spirit and restore me to rude health, the visiting nurse arranges regular family health checks at the Gatty Hall, in Ecclesfield, in a deliberate attempt to encourage me outdoors. Moderately impressive in its own right, the large stone building resembles an old school house but, situated across the road from the magnificent church of St. Mary, the Gatty Hall is permanently overshadowed.

Facing in the opposite direction, the church's large, rectangular windows are like magnets to the sun and when its glorious rays slope over the top of the Black Bull public house opposite, its beautiful stained glass windows are set ablaze within their arched stone frames and a flood of rainbow colours fall across the solemn congregation. Rising from a flat roof edged with alternate crenelles and rising spirals of stone, a massive bell tower hosts giant brass bells sombrely striking the hour throughout the day, reminding locals of its presence. Occasionally tolling the death knell of some eminent departed, its mournful chimes ring out the news, but, on Sunday and times of celebration, it melodiously calls the faithful to prayer from miles around. Tirelessly ticking away the years, the church's large round-faced clock has witnessed many treading a winding path to seek sanctuary behind huge wooden doors set in an imposing stone arch looking over a grassy cemetery. Keeping silent vigil over marble and stone memorials, engraved headstones and sunken, weather-beaten graves, beautiful stained-glass windows peer over a high stone wall beyond, towards tiny stone cottages and the occasional house-windowed shop nestling in its shadows on the far side of a cobbled road. Even the large, angular Black Bull opposite is rendered miniature by its dominance but, with piety on one side of the road, insobriety on the other, both the religious and sacrilegious walk the same path for a while. Some of the more pious shake their head in disgust on hearing raucous voices and bawdy music escaping into the street from the Black Bull as they tread a solemn path between gravestones to the church door. When a peel of bells toll the end of the prayers and members of the congregation leave the arched entrance to the sombre tones of the church organ, worshippers make their way home in contemplative mood subdued by the serious message delivered from the pulpit. When the huge gong above the bar in the Black Bull calls time on the evening's revelry, patrons pour onto the street in high spirits, their good-natured banter and singing echoing across the night.

The church's dismal graveyard almost defeats the purpose of the nearby clinic in the Gatty Hall, meant to improve the health and lift the spirits of the needy. Shaded by giant oaks and elms, it sends a firm reminder of mortality, prompting morbid thought and, once the children have been tended and large bottles of Cod Liver Oil and Malt lie in the depths of a grubby shopping bag, that graveyard beckons. Automatically slipping through the lych gate, I sit on a wooden form looking over the dismal sprawl and, while Carol and Celia playfully weave amongst the gravestones and Angela fitfully sleeps in the bucket pram, I mournfully reminisce among the dead.

Finally gathering my brood around me, I wander slowly amongst huge stone slabs set in the earth, occasionally resting to read poignant messages on my way to the cemetery gates, and curious onlookers might think some dear friend or relative is buried there because I shed desperate tears at each graveside reminding me of an innocent child's short life. Pausing in front of the church I stand visually tracing each line to its highest point, silently appealing to the Lord for help but secretly, I know there is no salvation.

Seven months after Angela's birth, familiar signs present themselves but I accept the news with grim resignation. No end to the pressure, a world already in turmoil begins steadily tipping off its axis and, at night, sitting alone in deteriorating surroundings, tears endlessly flow while I ponder on the purpose of life.

His interest in home and family diminished almost to the point of non-existence, Harry escapes the mayhem of mismanagement, leaving no clues as to his whereabouts. Long absences fuel dangerous thoughts and the scent of Ashes of Violets still lingering in memory, a potent cocktail of emotions tax my troubled mind, all-consuming jealousy holds me on the edge of a precipice.

In the midst of personal despair, glorious celebrations herald the end of the war. Red, white and blue bunting and Union Jacks fly from buildings all around Sheffield. People dance, sing and throw street parties but, while others fill with hope for a peaceful world, I hover on the brink of a black hole and by the time Janice is born, I am tipping over. No physical energy to tend the demanding newly-born, mental capacity for nurturing growing girls or inclination to steer the boys towards maturity, everything is overwhelming and even with the assistance of Social Services, family life is swiftly deteriorating. The able left to their own devices, dependent neglected, everything is plunging into a dreadful state of neglect and, amidst turmoil, the newly born screams night and day, depriving me of restful sleep. Trapped in a world of confusion I set in motion a chain of fear, with my hysterical demands for peace and my latest failing to thrive, nervous neglected children face the world with haunted expression, disturbed youths escape into the home of friends.

Suspicion clouds every day and, Harry flying free as a bird, wild obsession drives me to burning precious energy in daily probing, but shadows of the asylum forever hanging over me, I desperately try to hang on. Undeniable proof falling into the palm of my hand, I stare aghast at the packet of 'number nines' unexpectedly fished out of the pocket of Harry's jacket, and my miserable world spins, sending me hurtling over the edge. A shrill piercing scream escaping, a scurrying band of concerned offspring race over the doorstep, but, crazed with fear, I rush by. Unkempt hair flying wildly in the breeze, wild eyes glaring, I take flight, brandishing the ultimate evidence and frantically yelling in my blind confusion. Harry immediately thinks a terrible tragedy has occurred when I career towards him the minute he turns into Fulmere Road. In my anguish the implications of my impulsive act escape me and throwing myself at Harry, I pummel his chest hurling a torrent of abuse, uncharacteristically punctuated with foul language. Prompted by the sudden, loud disturbance neighbours peer from front windows some hurriedly making their way in the direction of the commotion, witnessing an assault so violent that building work across the road comes to a sudden halt and horrified workmen are forced to rush to Harry's aid.

Seized by madness giving me the strength of many, I frantically resist every attempt to restrain but, suddenly mindful of the consequences of my manic behaviour, I freeze. Immediately meek, apologetic and desperately afraid, racking sobs punctuate my hysterical explanation but, the mark of the asylum stamped large, a young man races along Fulmere Road and soon a trundling Black Maria arrives in advance of his return.

In a deeply melancholic state, I turn my back on the world on my return to the South Yorkshire Lunatic Asylum, and a battery of electric charges and stupor-inducing medication steadily reduce my capacity for rational thought. Slowly I become a bone fide member of that strange community once so desperately feared, returning home a seriously damaged individual with little connection to the real world and placing an extra burden on a family already struggling to cope.

Tears only a word away, I exist on another plain and, a bedraggled sight with no energy nor inclination for daily toil, slouch in the armchair by the hearth immediately on rising, viewing the world through a huge black cloud, family life carrying on without me. Forced to pick up the reins, Harry flounders under the multiple demands of home and, children and the newly born relentlessly screaming, he lays her in the crook of my arm in the vain hope that natural maternal instincts might come to the fore and bind us together. Sensing the distance between us, Janice merely kicks and screams, demanding attention denied her from the day of her birth, but, maternal instincts driven out by multiple pressures of years, I merely look down on my latest with frantic eyes, nothing left to offer.

Construction work devouring the open countryside outside our window appears to be sent to torment, and cement mixers drumming and whirring, machinery droning, diggers and drills whining and screeching, the wild cacophony drains away any remaining semblance of inner peace. Snapping the final chord, the shrill, piercing shriek of a hammer drill rips through the air and, clamping trembling hands tightly to my ears, I attempt to shut out the awful sound but Janice's mind-numbing screams penetrate my very soul. Blindly leaping to my feet, I send the innocent newly born hurtling to the floor, her anguished cries bringing an anxious Harry to the scene and the wrong conclusion. Immune to his ranting accusations I fall to my knees in front of the wireless, pleading for help from strangers communicating over the airwaves and, the arrival of a chugging Austin 10 motor car coincides with that of a trundling black van, its shaded windows denying the sun and prying eyes.

Flinging open its doors, two male nurses swiftly swing into action, running in advance of two solemn-faced doctors. Anxiously peering out from the front doorstep, Harry frantically gesticulates on their approach and, picking up desperate vibes, Janice writhes and screams in the crook of his arm, tiny fingers urgently clutching at the air. Uniformed strangers barging in, a curtain of fear falls over the living room. Recoiling in horror, Carol and Celia stealthily sidle along the back wall. Stuffing a tiny fist into her mouth Angela slinks in their wake stifling a cry of terror in a bid to escape attention. Swiftly grabbing her by the arm, Carol hauls her alongside into the shelter of darkness beneath the table. Stunned by the speed of things, three boys silently stand inside the kitchen doorway watching terrifying events unfold.

Locked in dialogue with the unseen, I automatically respond to the encouragement of nursing staff, gently easing me to my feet, but the menacing sight of the Black Maria standing outside the front window instantly catapults me back into reality. Seized by a fit of hysteria, survival instincts kick in and, kicking, screaming and spewing hysterical accusations at Harry, I wage a desperate battle to escape and their grip tightens, but in my deranged state, superhuman strength temporarily keeps them at bay until clamped into a strait jacket I stand there trussed as a chicken, cowed in defeat. Hauled towards the open door I throw a final glance over my shoulder, terrified at the sight of two doctors leaning over a document on the table, knowing that their illegible signatures are legally committing me to the asylum. Numb with shock, I stare, blankly, through shaded windows as the Black Maria carries me away from Fulmere Road and home disappears into the distance.

Faces drained Peter, Steven and Michael stare into the empty street from the front window, beneath the table Carol and Celia crawl further into the darkness, Angela wets her underclothes in fear and, curled in a silent ball against Harry's chest, Janice attempts to hide from the terrifying world she has inherited. Outside in the street, huddled groups watch the departing vehicle, heads shaking in despair, the whole train of events indelibly etched on their minds. Frock coat brushing the surface of his shoes, prayer book in hand, Father Mahoney hurries along Fulmere Road, too late to comfort a distraught, tormented member of his flock or four screaming children being coaxed into a car by Social Service staff.

CHAPTER ELEVEN
TRAPPED

Huge wooden doors menacingly beckoning, tiers of barred windows screaming of lost freedoms, the huge clock on the clock tower mocks those indoors with no need for the time in their caged existence, and, instinctively I sense the old chapter of my life ending, a new, more sinister, one about to begin.

Flight instincts kicking in, I struggle against attempts to haul me indoors, valiantly battle against enforced admittance and resist every inch of the way along white-walled corridors, whispering of decades of suffering, but. shackled, my desperate efforts are futile. In the powerful grip of daily tranquillisers, inmates stroll aimlessly, clothing askew, cigarettes drooping from partially opened mouths, dribbling with uncontrolled salivation and, despite its name changed from South Yorkshire Lunatic Asylum to Middlewood Hospital, the frightening place is still bedlam. Freed from the straitjacket and thrust into a padded cell for my determined resistance, I panic and, four walls closing in, I can barely breathe. Gaining strength from raw fear I frantically beat clenched fists against a heavy padlocked door wailing as a banshee in my desperation, but padded cells, in isolation, it's no use. Drained of tears I anxiously peer through a tiny grid in the heavily-reinforced door and the same wild look in their eye, others, peering through the same iron grids opposite, tell me I am not alone in my despair.

Tortured by the sheer injustice of it all, physically and mentally weakened by battle, I fling myself on the basic single bed in the corner of the cell but, darkness closing in, my imagination feeds on the movement of my own shadow flitting, ghostly, around the walls as I pace the cell throughout the long, lonely night. Every waking moment a living nightmare, I desperately fight for freedom and, yelling abuse at captors, screaming wild accusations of Harry's unfaithfulness. I know they think it is all in my mind and regular spells in the padded cell becomes the norm. Only narrow grids in the locked door give me sight of the occasional human being passing by, but, as yet, no daylight has brought Harry. Not a word from home; it is a lonely and terrifying existence faced with the knowledge that the law has forcefully committed me here. Nagging fears of permanent imprisonment drive me to bouts of crazy, inane wailing and I sometimes doubt my own sanity locked in this vacuum of helplessness, but what can I do: nobody to speak on my behalf and explain how circumstances have brought me to this point?

No longer any meaning to life, I return their food, knowing I will eventually have no choice but to succumb to their brutal force feeding, but I fear more the prospect of a long time in this madhouse than the possibility of death. Over endless days avidly searching the corridor outside, keenly listening for approaching footsteps, all hope is fading, but, two faces appearing at the grille in the cell door, I stop dead, eyes gaping. Certain I have been drawn into some wild hallucination, I shake my head in a bid to remove the scene from my eyes, because there stands Harry, a young woman by his side. Fires of hell burning in my eyes, hair unkempt, I leap forward jabbing a quivering finger in the direction of the woman young enough to be Harry's daughter. Urgently gasping for air, I thrust a trembling hand between the grids in a vain bid to grasp the lapel of Harry's jacket and, face draining, the young woman makes a frantic bid to escape, but Harry holds her there. My probing eyes flit up and down a mass of rich auburn hair swept high above her forehead, open calf-length coat exposing a smart pin-striped suit with the wide collar of a sparkling white blouse overlaying the lapels of her jacket, and there is no doubt she is attractive but, seeing only a vixen with claws sunk into Harry, my grasping hand reaches in her direction.

Saliva dribbling from the corners of my mouth, fingers blanched, I frantically shake the grid in the cell door in a desperate bid to vent my uncontrollable fury. Gently explaining that the young woman had agreed to be his paid housekeeper, looking after things at home in my absence, Harry attempts to placate me, but, picking up the scent of Ashes of Violets drifting from her person, I search her pallid face and, jealousy all-consuming, wild inane ramblings escape. Face contorted with rage, eyes wide with disbelief, skin a sickly pallor, I cling to the grid more tightly when my legs begin to crumble and, a blood-curdling scream reverberating around the cell, their scurrying footsteps quickly fade into the distance.

Slumping, distraught against the cell door, my face carelessly pressed against the grille, I stare despairingly along the empty corridor and, finally collapsing in a crumpled heap, frantically beat the padded floor with an open palm. Eventually curling in foetal position, I sob uncontrollably but there is no-one there to witness my terrible suffering. Successive shock treatments and calming medication eventually find me on the open ward, a pathetic sight. A robot under the influence of powerful drugs, adult reduced to infantile behaviour, I walk around in a dazed state, a far cry from the proud, artistic Alice of old. Tremendous damage done, I shuffle around the ward, dress careless, stockings wrinkled around my ankles, toilet habits clumsy and head shaking, jabber in baby tongue.

Through barred windows I watch seasons come and go but, emotions blunted by medication, see the world only in shades of black and grey. Though spring encourages buds to life, summer brings the flowers, autumn turns the leaves of giant trees lining the pathway to various shades of orange and brown and winter brings the snow, I feel no enthusiasm for the changing scene. Another year turning, there is still no sign of Harry and, distancing myself from the crazy world around, I fester in some quiet corner, my head filled only with thoughts of home. Each unbearable day, I wonder how much longer I can endure life in this hell-hole with no news to lift my spirits or allay concerns about children left behind.

Deeply melancholic, I dwell on dark thoughts and know my constant weeping and wailing is hindering chances of release but, in more rational moments, silently brood, strangely wondering whether I misconstrued things in the first place in my deeply depressed post-natal state. Whether the young woman was innocent after all and simply being generous in offering to look after my home. Still, no matter how hard I try, I can find no answer to the haunting question of the mysterious 'Number Nine' secretly tucked in Harry's jacket pocket.

Spring is becoming a blur. Only strangers, daily travelling the winding driveway beyond the barred window, I am beginning to panic. Nurses in stiffened white hats, dark capes draped around their shoulders, ending their night shift and eagerly returning to families. Others hurrying in chattering groups towards the wooden doors, ready to begin the next. Doctors, surgeons, matrons, consultants, domestic staff coming and going while I remain imprisoned here, envious of their freedom and terrified I might never regain mine.

Still more weeks drag by, but no Harry. The sun at its height we should be strolling down country lanes as a family now, treading fields, meadows and open moorland as in those hazy days gone by.

Collecting wild flowers, making daisy chains, picking wild fruit and breathing in fresh air, not constantly inhaling smoke of self-made cigarettes to ease my boredom and wile away endless days. Absorbing the sweet scent of blossoms, not the unpleasant odour of stale urine and faeces drifting from the incontinent. Listening to the mating call of birds in their pairing, not anguished wails of tortured souls or battle cries of the despairing, venting their frustration on the equally troubled. Watching lambs gambol in green fields, not drugged, moronic people wandering aimlessly through pointless lives. Tasting freedom, not the bitter pill of captivity. The treadmill forever turning, I feel I will never again feel solid ground. Days are again growing shorter and, still shunning company, I am going crazy with longing to see home and family but, tortured by vivid imaginings of someone else already living there, my weight is plummeting and I am struggling to hold on. Each day sinking further into a dark abyss, I finally give in and responding to no-one in my despair, I am putty in the hands of men in white coats hauling me off for cruel treatments merely numbing the heartache without eradicating the cause, because I fear strange things are afoot at Fulmere Road.

The scene might be festive, but Christmas does nothing except highlight long alienation from my family. Tinsel and baubles trim the asylum, richly decorated Christmas trees bring life to dismal wards, seasonal sermons in the chapel tell of a wondrous God offering succour and support for the suffering, but nothing lifts my spirits. Nurses in seasonal attire walk the wards, lanterns swinging, singing carols of old and, for a while, there is a change in the atmosphere but, time of hope and goodwill only temporary, tomorrow will be just another miserable day. Another twenty-four hours to add to the many I've spent living in hope of eventual freedom, but it has been such a long time and I have ploughed so many lonely furrows, no relatives visiting. Wept so many tears, fought so many pointless battles both mental and physical, strength is waning, and pottering around the wards offering a helping hand, there is growing acceptance that patience might be the best policy.

I am over the moon with excitement. My calmer mood bringing surprising dividends I am being recommended for home leave! However, I am a little concerned. Having been to hell and back, there is no doubt I have changed beyond all recognition. Drawn, haunted face reflecting the pain of rejection, incarceration and cruel, inhuman treatments, my character has taken a battering and I have grown bitter and cynical. Since the initial burst of euphoria, I have had time to think, at times viewing the prospect of freedom with some trepidation. The outside world hostile, and wary of ex-inmates of the asylum roaming the streets, I will be destined to always walk under a shadow. Regarded as dangerous by some, idiot ripe for mocking by others, simply because of my time here. Nevertheless, my experience has strangely served me well, because gradually creating a barrier of steel against life's cruelties, I have survived experiences capable of breaking even the most robust human spirit, and with my protective shield around me I will again face the world. Unexpectedly, the thought of at last seeing offspring long left behind almost breaks it down. Their faces indelibly etched in memory, it pains me to think mine might be forgotten and that I will simply be a stranger to the tiny infant I barely knew, distresses me to realise important milestones in their lives have, inevitably, passed by without my involvement. Yet, will I even recognise my own flesh and blood so many years having past since sight of them? Adults now, what influences in their lives have formed their passage to maturity, serving to cement for them a decent, secure future, or have those painful younger years left mental wounds far too deep to heal? A flood of emotions threatening to thwart my chance of freedom, I lower the barrier with fresh determination, dismissing worrying thoughts of Harry and the woman once accompanying him.

Self-control the key to my release, I brace myself, presenting a calm, amenable individual to the Board of Control and, displaying no signs of inner turmoil, successfully gain permission for a short period of leave. Brushing reservations aside, I am finally looking forward to going home. For the first time since my incarceration I feel stirrings of life and, standing by the dormitory window, I swear the sun takes on a bright shade of yellow, the grass a rich mixture of greens, and that waving branches of trees along the winding pathway warmly welcome me back to the world.

Freedom only hours away, I can hardly contain my excitement making my way to Sister Hetherington's office but, immediately on opening the door, I feel an overwhelming sense of unease. White starched apron over a smart navy-blue dress with stiffly starched white collar and cuffs, a neat white cap sits proudly on curly black hair but, a weak smile barely lifting the corners of her mouth, Sister Hetherington is clearly uncomfortable. The atmosphere grave, I am immediately overcome by a dark feeling of impending doom and my legs wobble, body trembles as she rises from the desk to greet me, an open palm inviting me to sit in the chair opposite. Instantly fearing some terrible tragedy has occurred at Fulmere Road, my heart races, imagination runs riot and, throat parched, I can barely swallow. Knowing I am not yet strong enough to cope with tragic family news, I search Sister Hetherington's face for reassurance but, averting her gaze, she appears extremely ill at ease, constantly shuffling papers around her desk, tapping them into a neat pile and placing them at the side of a letter written in familiar style. Expression solemn, she rises from the chair, the intriguing letter raised in front of her face and, head shaking in seeming disbelief, repeatedly scans its content. Instinctively, I know she is about to deliver something unpalatable. Resting with her back against the table in front of me, her worried gaze meets mine and I almost feel her mental pain as she presses a comforting arm on mine in a vain attempt to soften the blow of being forced to deliver what can only be distressing news. In no fit state to take any more of life's cruelties, I grab her arm but, the impact finally striking home, I frantically search the room for means of escape. My feet merely treading water I make a clumsy attempt to dash for the door, but physical strength immediately deserting me, I slump, helplessly, back on the chair. Things frozen in time I sit dazed, blankly staring into space, cruel words screaming inside my head and I instinctively know this is the final straw destroying the road to recovery. In my mind's eye, I see a vision of myself running along a long, dark tunnel attempting to reach the light but only a black void stretches ahead. Unable to grasp the horror of it all I silently pray Sister Hetherington will soon revoke her words and tell me it's not true, but the thin line of her lips and moist eyes tell me of her own despair on my behalf, grim expression leaves me in no doubt the news is inescapable reality. Harry has refused to have me back.

Four walls closing in, I desperately gasp for air, and, a piercing scream of sheer terror suddenly reverberating around the room, dashing footsteps pound the echoing corridor outside. Concerned members of staff bursting into the room, I blindly throw caution to the wind, threshing around in their firm grasp, striking out in all directions and venting my fears on the innocent in my desperate bid for freedom, but the odds are against me and, clamped in a straitjacket, hauled off to a padded cell, I am back to square one. Thrust into the suffocating space, I desperately plead for release but, the huge key turning in the lock, I know from long, painful experience there will be no escape. Faced with the alarming news and the prospect of a life of incarceration, not even that carefully-constructed suit of armour can protect me now. Distraught at my abandonment, wild with anger and crazy with disbelief, I am totally inconsolable and finally almost going insane with the sheer injustice of it all.

Dangerous in my temporary madness, I verbally lash out at approaching staff, innocently going on their daily rounds, but a battery of powerful narcotics and electric shocks play havoc with any remaining normality and I walk around the wards in a wooden state, a subservient member of a strange community, surviving each day amongst precious memories. In my unbalanced state, strange visions become seeming normality and, voices whispering in my ear, I respond in animated fashion, gesticulating into fresh air and responding in hushed tone.

Every pointless day plunging me further into a downward spiral, I finally sink into a deep slough of despair and nothing can lift me from my melancholy state. Worried by my total withdrawal from the world, concerned staff provide wool, knitting needles and sewing equipment in an attempt to encourage useful activity and, working, clockwork fashion, I gradually craft a growing mountain of hats, gloves, scarves and rag dolls for children left behind, jealously guarding them in my struggle to keep hope alive, but a dusty pile of gifts merely serve as a permanent reminder of the pointless task and my rejection. Yet, how can I make this awful place my permanent home? No power over my life or privacy in which to grieve, I will forever remain a statistic – Alice Watson Patient Number 2549 – a prisoner secured as if a murderous criminal detained in H.M. Prison. Mere cushions protecting me from reality, drugs might dull the mind and calm erratic behaviour, but they are no substitute for the real world left behind, no replacement for home and family or permanent cure for the dreadful pain of heartache and loss and, the future too terrifying to contemplate, I can't take any more. No further need for the straitjacket, padded cell or shock treatment, my battling days are over and, tucked away in some secluded corner, I will survive each day in a melancholic vacuum, mentally dwelling on happier times. Locked deep in my head, nobody can take those precious memories away and even the most determined has no power greater than mine if I choose to stay inside this cocoon and refuse to let them in. My only private space in this living hell, I will stay here until death claims me.

Inexplicably escorted to a waiting vehicle, I watch the world go by through shaded windows, eyes blank, familiar sights along

Middlewood Road highlighting my alienation from the world. Women pushing prams serve as a painful reminder of happier times, playful children of lost offspring, couples holding hands tell me that life goes on regardless of my absence. No more emotions left to inflict pain, sorrow or gladness, no tears to shed any more for what is gone because inside I am dying and willingly fading away. Even sight of the old Royal Infirmary fails to rouse my long-held fears of institutions because, as a lamb led to slaughter, I know I will have no choice but to succumb to their treatments and, soon wheeled into an operating theatre, I am already resigned.

Staff in green v-neck short-sleeve cotton jackets and matching draw-string trousers mill around the room, a huge, glaring light above a pristine operating table sets alight a tray of gleaming equipment neatly laid out on a tray alongside my bed. Although grown used to mental and physical probing, I am strangely afraid at the sight of a surgeon, in surgical 'greens' and tie-back cloth hat, coming to a halt alongside me. Facial mask hiding his identity, he leans over me and I have an overwhelming sense of dread in my helpless state, but, as the anaesthetist bends to his task, I fall calm because I know death will not be the worst outcome. Indeed, why fear death when faced with the alternative of survival and a life lived within a waking nightmare? With luck on my side, I might never wake again. Drilling holes either side of my forehead, the surgeon gains access to my brain, inserting electrodes and firing them at frontal lobes in an experimental pre-frontal leucotomy. Severing vital memory cells holding me in the past, he takes a dangerous gamble with my future.

Returned to the asylum, I exist in another guise, dress careless, stockings wrinkled around my ankles and, strangely at ease in the role, walk with shoulders pulled well back in a stiff strut exhibiting a contradictory sense of pride. Strangely speaking with refined diction, I view the world through blank eyes. Every vowel exaggerated, word stretched in an affected manner, a strange smile lights my face as if bemused by the world, and my whole persona reflects the peculiar character surgeons have created. Drugs finally stabilise me but terrible, irreversible damage has been done, yet there is no-one to grieve the passing of that old me. Nobody to mourn her loss, no marker in some sheltered spot telling the world in which she had existed, loved and been loved, no-one to pay homage to the old Alice who will never again see the light of day. A mere shell of a human being with malfunctioning brain, scars are visible but, grown used to the asylum now, a great void separates me from the past and life starts anew.

Alone in the world, I am destined to travel life's road to its end in the company of its casualties. People with troubled minds, malformed bodies or who life itself has weakened and destroyed, soldiers whose last sighting of the world had been of a bloody battlefield seen through a blinding flash, sounds, the deafening thunder of exploding bombs and mines. Too damaged to enjoy freedoms won, traumatised servicemen unfairly spend their days in the same cruel environment, the stigma of the asylum wrapped around them. Once pride of the nation, men sleep in long dormitories with only a single locker between each bed, no private space in which to muse, be spared indignities or find the peace of mind necessary to heal the mental wounds of war.

Now reduced to a mental cripple, I finally join the ranks of bona-fide members of the asylum's strange community, readily accepting and seemingly comfortable amongst others with similarly unpredictable personalities. Deprived of the niceties of life, I assume the same magpie tendencies, sneaking away items left around and bartering them for cigarettes or trinkets taking my fancy. A life crutch and imperative, drugs keep me in check in my semi-normal state, but there is no miracle capable of bringing back the old Alice. A guinea pig for the world of science, intriguing experiment for the medical profession, the repercussions of their deed are yet to unfold.

CHAPTER TWELVE
CLOSURE

Dreadful impersonal conditions and forced incarceration of the abandoned and forgotten has sparked outrage and a curious world begins looking through the windows of the asylum. Built in sprawling grounds, a new workshop begins preparing inmates for freedom, and, shackles falling away, the whole ethos of the place is changing. In this more optimistic atmosphere, with the past having been laid to rest, I find a new spur. Middle-aged, neat and calm, I work robotically alongside others, making useful goods for sale, proving dexterous and willing and eventually being placed with an employer, taking part in a scheme to re-introduce inmates to the world and semi-independence. Deep indents, either side of my forehead, the only visible signs of damage done, I daily catch the bus to a cutlery firm at the head of The Moor, leaving behind the tag of insanity at the asylum gates.

Strutting gait and strange, distant smile accepted as merely quirky, only isolating insecurity sets me apart from the bustling throng. Sadly, brain-damaged, I quickly prove a drain on other workers in my need for constant supervision, but the exercise is only aborted when a hoard of stolen items is discovered in my locker. For too long the asylum has been my home, cunning, my means of survival in a world where equally deprived patients squirrel away personal belongings carelessly left around.

Back in the cloistered walls of the asylum, I am routinely assigned to supervised duties around the wards, in the laundry or in cramped dormitories in order to reawaken long-lost domestic skills necessary for survival in the outside world. Yet, strangely, after all these miserable years, the asylum has finally become my normality and captors having won. I have no desire for life outside its walls, but unexpected news wings its way along the grapevine. Apparently, letters have been despatched to, sometimes long-lost, relatives in the hope of creating even the flimsiest thread to the outside world prior to the asylum's closure; but for some, there is nobody to welcome them back. The outside world tainted by bigotry and cruelty, the traumatic road will be littered with obstacles and I am filled with foreboding at every step, but signs of dismantling already visible beds stand empty, inmates tread echoing corridors for the last time.

From the dormitory window I watch their departure, some bewildered, others clearly lifted at the prospect of a new life after long years of incarceration, but their world will never be the same as the one left behind all that time ago. Cruel treatments and medication changing mental and physical processes, people will readily recognise the signs resulting from daily doses of drugs keeping them calm and the public safe from sometimes erratic behaviour, and the cord will never be broken. Soon it will be my turn and my rock over so many years, Sister Hetherington, takes me under her wing, supervising me in domestic duties in her own home in preparation for life in the unfamiliar world outside, but my mind damaged beyond repair, it's a daunting task. Numbers around me dwindling, now I have no appetite to face alone the outside world, no home or family waiting. Unexpectedly summoned to her office, Sister Hetherington is visibly thrilled to impart the news that she has contacted my old home with a view to possible family reconciliation, but mention of home stirs no memories of the place, nor people living there. In any case, while I have grown used to the asylum, the building itself will surely deter visitors from venturing up the driveway.

The worst time of year for first sighting of the place, its awesome sprawl rears, menacingly, through autumn mists, black clouds overhead cast the grounds in darkness, fierce winds eddy and scream around its ancient stone, and from high on the clock tower, the ghostly face of the clock peers down on the miserable scene. From barred windows, expressionless faces look towards the uncertain future worryingly beckoning, and a daunting sight for first-time visitors, it might serve to deter even the bravest of souls.

Activities known only to those working and unfortunate enough to reside there, weird stories have long circulated outside its perimeter. Its very name transporting minds into frightening realms of fantasy, maybe people will be afraid to beat a path to my door, dubious of meeting a long-term inmate of bedlam, petrified that I might harbour violent tendencies.

If only I could allay their fears, welcome them at the door and escort them around familiar corridors to the ladies' ward introducing them to remaining inmates, long my only companions in the world. Explain how some have been reduced to madness by circumstances overturning their world.

No doubt Kate Palfreyman would frighten them with that wild look in her eyes, but I could tell them it only reflects her anger at life and inability to cope with a disturbed childhood, abusive teenage years and violent marriage.

That, transported onto another plain by the tragic loss of a young child and both her parents on the same day, Maureen Brown simply refuses to let go and, walking the ward 'cooing' and whispering into the ear of an imaginary child cradled in her arms, she is merely seeking relief from dreadful heartache in fantasy.

Who knows what befell Emma Turner? A young woman tortured by wild imaginings, constantly talking gibberish to the wall. Emma might worry them, but I could let them know she is a gentle soul and incapable of harming a fly.

Curled, in a foetal ball, in the depths of an armchair, face creased in a toothless grin, inane laughter occasionally escaping, life has simply taken its toll on old Freda Earnshaw and, calling to parents long gone from the world, she looks frail in her senility and not long for this.

Constantly weeping and wailing Sylvia Peacock and Doris Major might upset them but they are merely victims of nature's quirks, fluctuating hormonal changes playing havoc with their sanity during menopause.

Suffering post-natal depression, young women have found themselves unable to cope with the pressures of a newborn, their irrational behaviour often brought about by the physical and mental demands of new motherhood, lack of physical support, extreme tiredness and changing hormones. Though a daily dose of tranquillisers somewhat eases their distress, making them easier to control, dramatic treatments have left their mark. Devoid of expression, strange, staring eyes and robotic movements reflect devastating effects.

Corridors stripped of troubled souls, wards almost empty now, only the sound of my footsteps echo through the silence on answering the call to Sister Hetherington's office. A curious smile playing around her plump lips, she greets me warmly as I enter, an outstretched hand directing my attention to two young ladies nervously hovering by the window. No chords to strike in my damaged brain, I blankly search their faces but, though similar features and build suggest the same stock, they are as strangers. Nevertheless, a strange affinity draws me towards them and I hold them close on learning they are two of my long-lost daughters, Angela and Janice, but no real connection, it is merely an act of good manners, because separate lives stand between us.

Beneath asylum shadows, we stroll through roaming grounds, sometimes sheltering in the gatehouse at the end of the drive to chat awhile but, despite attempts to revive memories, my past is almost irretrievably erased, and life has to begin again. Though recall occasionally and unexpectedly flits across my mind, it is gone in a flash and their life, as much a mystery to me as mine to them, I have nothing to contribute to their small talk as they speak of days long gone now. Of troubled years under the iron, often cruel, rule of a stepmother named Sally, twenty years their father's junior, arriving in their midst at the age of twenty-one, shortly after my enforced incarceration. Her sudden arrival sparking a flurry of local gossip, some neighbours were bitter, others openly hostile, deliberately shunning her when a self-explanatory bulge at her waistline quickly grew to huge proportions.

Others kept a critical eye on events on the girls' return from the Children's Homes. Moments of bitterness, frustration and extreme anger sometimes punctuating their story, it's clear they had endured an unhappy and neglected home life under Sally's care. Yet even in its telling, pure human instinct drives me to react only as a stranger with no maternal attachment or loyalty to my own, instead feeling unexpected sympathy and a measure of understanding for that young woman when they speak of their father living a virtual bachelor life, shrugging off all family responsibility and handing it lock, stock and barrel to Sally. Strangely, I momentarily feel an affinity and understanding for her frustration and ever-changing moods under the weight of such heavy responsibility at such a young age. Yet sympathy is tinged with sadness and perhaps a hint of anger at the effect her behaviour had on my girls in their formative years.

Events, it seemed had also had devastating effect on my boys because apparently, Peter and Steven resented her intrusion in their lives, things sometimes verging on the confrontational, resulting in a dysfunctional, discordant family. Life had thrown Michael into a different, more alien, world. Removed from home, by the Local Authorities, he escaped his traumatic family life and, placed in a boarding school, he entered one of higher education, strict discipline and imposed social values, often at variance to the ones he had known, slowly distancing him from his Yorkshire working-class roots and previous life of trouble and poverty. Eventually, well-educated and aspirational, his sights were set on a higher plain on his return home. Drafted into National Service in his absence, Peter and Steven merely flitted in and out of the family home, its atmosphere far from conducive to happiness and contentment and, eventually 'signing on,' they left behind those troubled years at Fulmere Road.

By the time of their return from the Children's Homes it seems time had erased all memories of my existence at Fulmere Road from the girl's minds, but, apparently, occasional secretive mutterings in the street and at home quickly led them to believe a skeleton lay hidden deep in the family cupboard. Alienated from the truth, childish curiosity and suspicion immediately distanced them from Sally when casually introduced by their father as their 'new mother'. At their own admission they were confused, insecure, nervous, uncommunicative and very difficult to handle. Sally five foot ten inches tall, they tiny for their age, she towered above them and, visibly, they were as chalk and cheese. No shared attributes, blood ties, past to bind, there was no warmth between them, only resentment at being thrust under the same roof. Sally's first child lost at birth, she soon harboured resentment at her captive state and, exploiting her height advantage, she ruled by fear until time forged an impenetrable barrier between them.

True maternal feelings naturally attaching her to her second born, the gap between them widened and, standing in the way of her ability to create her own small family unit, she rendered them servile and submissive. Scrubbing floors on hands and knees, running errands, babysitting, lighting coal fires, their young lives were filled with adult activity and, a huge hand leaving bright red weals across legs and faces at less than perfection, they flinched at her every approach and the seeds of mutual dislike were soon deeply sown. Pale, thin and cowed they attracted the attention of concerned neighbours but, foiling their curiosity, Sally's cruel deeds were done behind closed doors with threats of retribution guaranteeing their silence. Poverty, cruelty and neglect dogging them daily, the birth of Sally's third born saw them eventually consigned to the outer edge of the family and, no drudgery for half-blood siblings, bitterness and resentment at their preferential treatment grew daily.

Although a virtual stranger in their lives, I listen with great sadness to their tale of how, showered with love and attention, those younger siblings thrived while they were cowed in the company of strangers. Yet they speak warmly of shared childhood days, nevertheless forging a thread between them. Physical and emotional abuse increasing through the years, the gap between Sally and themselves grew wider and, differences irreconcilable, rebelliousness set in during teenage years. The house turned into a war zone, they vented the fury of years, becoming embroiled in ferocious verbal and physical battles with Sally. Taking the easy route and alienating the girls from his life, their father defended Sally without question and, a distance forged between them, every hour became just another welcome step on the road to their departure from Fulmere Road.

In more reflective moments, Carol and Celia somewhat resentfully view things with maturity, recognising the huge burden of responsibility Sally carried over the years and that, struggling by on a pittance, she had drawn the short straw in the marital relationship. Shoulders stooped with the weight of it all, rich auburn hair greying, years of toil and struggle etched in her once handsome face, she had become a bitter harridan. In sharp contrast, the years had been kind to their father and his first brood having flown the nest, he now thrives in the bosom of his new family. Split into two halves, a new branch of the Watson family has taken root on Fulmere Road and the old has been lopped.

Piece by piece the girls fit together the jigsaw of those troubled years and I feel great sadness at my forced absence from their lives, but, yesterday lived without me, there are no shared trials, tribulations, heartache or happiness forming bonds over the years. Nevertheless, time slowly forging a tenuous connection between us, we may still find common ground, new things yet to be painted on that blank canvas.

In the outside world, my calm exterior and quiet, gentle manner gives the impression of normality, but though time has naturally delivered a middle-aged woman to the world, man's interference with vital organs has created a strange phenomenon and, once shadows of the asylum fall away, a Pandora's Box sometimes opens and an unpredictable personality emerges. One minute a magnet to strangers with my automatic smile, friendly personality and agreeable nature, the next an alarming individual muttering urgent claims of spiders crawling around inside my head, bees entering my ears and snakes writhing around in my stomach. Sometimes lucid and articulate, complete gibberish occasionally escapes, innocently worrying many. A temporary blip, the triggering mechanism quickly corrects itself and seeming normality gains me acceptance in the outside world.

Over time, I meet other estranged children and though scant memory of my part in their lives, my younger girls become regular visitors to the asylum but, her own life plagued with problems, Carol has more urgent pressures on her time and has no wish to increase them by dredging up the bitter past.

Having discovered life beyond the family home Michael has found his own escape in things educational and future success. Desperate to close the door on the past and leave years of heartache on the shores of England, Peter chose to 'let sleeping dogs lie,' deliberately settling in a far-flung corner of the world, making New Zealand his home in the hope of erasing, forever, painful memories, long blighting his life.

Sadly, I have no past in which to dip and recall memories of the handsome young man in army uniform, a black beret pressed on jet black wavy hair, but Sister Hetherington tells me he is my son, Steven. Though trained to fight the most brutal of enemies, our reunion instantly breaks down his guard and, face crumbling, he struggles for control. Unable to see the mother he once knew beyond my strange exterior, he breaks down sobbing, like a baby, in my arms because it is clear I have become a programmed, obedient product of cruel medical intervention and long years of institutional living. Throughout the reconciliation I smile, vacantly, automatically slotting yet another stranger into my life.

Soon, I meet grandchildren I have never known, on equal terms, because each is a stranger to the other. Mere babes in arms and toddlers, readily accepting, with childish innocence, they see only the person I have become and we slowly build bridges. Futures set to merge, an unfamiliar sense of belonging is gradually stirring. My home for two decades now, I wander around the asylum, an empty shell robbed of the capacity to effectively function in the unfamiliar outside world frighteningly beckoning me back. Corridors silent, wards almost empty, members of staff help me pack what few personal belongings I have managed to accumulate over the years and, taking a final lingering look around, I feel a strange nostalgia for the familiar. A hasty glance over my shoulder captures a full view of the asylum as the car moves away and today the sun is catching its many windows but there are no longer inmates to peer, longingly, outward. Huge wooden doors shut me out now instead of locking me in, but the clock high on the clock tower remains to monotonously tick away the hours. Half past three! Time to go now, but I am afraid!

CHAPTER THIRTEEN
FREEDOM AT LAST

Specially built to accommodate long-term inmates released from the asylum, the angular, red-brick, complex stands on the brow of a hill at Southey Green overlooking a distant, panoramic view of glorious countryside and the massive sprawl of Parson Cross. Nevertheless, after years of enclosed living, endless space is overwhelming and, despite a measure of warden care, I struggle with semi-independence, seeking relief from boredom in pointless wanderings. Lost, lonely and afraid I face an alien world, missing the security of the asylum and those with whom I had spent so many years because, escaping one trap, I have been plunged into another. Strangers milling around unfamiliar streets, once trundling traffic arriving at speed, from all directions, horns toot at my jaywalking and, nervous, I cross roads at my peril. Twenty years with little financial responsibility has left me ill-prepared for the dramatic leap to financial independence and I am more bewildered than most by the new decimal coinage, simply opening my purse and placing trust in shop assistants on purchasing cigarettes.

Amidst daily confusion, I find comfort in the friendliness of local people chatting, at will, to strangers on my lonely travels, but a chance encounter triggers a spark. Approaching a huge, red-brick, building at the foot of Southey Hill, I stop dead in my wanderings, studying, with quizzical gaze, fluted concrete over a stone canopy overhanging huge wooden doors. A colourful billboard advertising the latest film, my eyes wander over a romantic scene and huge letters writ large over the stone canopy alongside – THE RITZ. A momentary memory flits, unexpectedly, across my mind. Unwittingly, during their reminiscences, my daughters had drawn for me a mental map of the place I once lived and, driven by curiosity, I embark on an impulsive journey searching for my lost yesterday. However, having learned from life's many pitfalls, I am wary and, twisting and turning with the roads, I thread amongst numerous houses making enquiries along the way, but Parson Cross is a huge, confusing estate. A clear landmark, the sprawling Parson Cross Hotel, rears before me, its colourful sign hanging from a tall pole on the edge of the yard, swaying in the breeze. Hurrying up Deerlands Avenue, I make a wrong left turn, finding myself confronted by a squat church nestled in a semi-circle of houses. Something stirs but it's fleeting and seeking directions from a frock-coated vicar speaking to a parishioner in the arched doorway, I retrace my steps. A metal sign, screaming from high on a corner house, tells me I am entering Fulmere Road.

Jubilantly trotting, my blank expression fools the world. Noses pressed close to the glass, elderly faces peer outward, mouths agape at my strutting approach and mentally counting down the numbers, I finally stand outside a red-brick house at the end of a terrace of four neat homes, vainly searching for memories long erased.

Under the startled gaze of a wizened face peering from the window alongside, I absorb every detail, but nothing prompts recall. Nevertheless it's clear that, over recent years, the front garden has been left to fall into a terrible state of neglect, and curving dry-stone walls are crumbling, grass overgrown, weeds flourishing. Hurrying down the pathway, I hear the sash window next door, thrust wide and can almost feel prying eyes tracking my progress. Entering the back porch, I rap sharply on the door but, nobody home, settle on the back step, looking over the long back garden, noting nature's steady reclamation. Tall grass and weeds gaining a firm hold, broken glass and disintegrating cold frame bear witness to past horticultural interest. Alongside a red-brick air raid shelter, wilting rhubarb rots, dry raspberry canes appear long past their fruiting, but a hardy gooseberry bush beneath the kitchen window still bears fruit.

Retracing my steps, I catch sight of the elderly lady leaning over the windowsill next door, sheer shock clouding her face as I tread a path across the garden towards the front window. Cupping my hands against the glass, I peer in, scanning the room for things familiar, but the neat interior stirs nothing of my past and, under her startled gaze, I strut, stiffly, back along Fulmere Road leaving it all behind. A pointless journey, it's all of some other time, some other life, long wiped from memory's page.

The one-off aberration a seeming harbinger of doom, Janice tells me their father has unexpectedly died from thrombosis! Though no more than a stranger, his death prompts strange thoughts, and, while the world sleeps, I lie awake in the tiny back bedroom of my daughter's home on the Shiregreen estate, pondering what might have been. The futility of my life bearing down, a torrent of useless tears gradually wash away my burden, but as darkness gradually gives way to light, morning finds me ready to face the world anew. Long trained to acceptance, a fixed smile hides the trials of the night, but black pouches beneath bulbous eyes bear silent witness.

Life in the outside world proving a terrifying and dangerous experience, freedom has set me another challenge. Outside the asylum I am a curio, a loner and a misfit, looking in on life but not living and, desperately lonely, I struggle through each miserable day, growing bored with a freedom, having nothing to offer, but then there is a strange and unexpected turn of events.

Armed only with second-hand knowledge, Steven's bereaved father-in-law, Stanley Barker, paints an unbiased picture on being introduced and, seeing only an inoffensive, softly-spoken individual he begins to occasionally take me out and together we find a new spark. Presenting a seemingly ordinary couple to the world, we walk, hand in hand, around the streets of Sheffield and, obedient and amiable, I fill the void in his life and the uncomplicated nature of the relationship keeps a lid on my unpredictable behaviour.

However, quickly deciding to take me into his home as a housekeeper, Stanley worries many, but when a sense of decency just as swiftly leads him to make a reckless decision to marry, some are dreadfully concerned. Once a long-term mental patient, so deranged as to be strapped in a straitjacket and committed to a padded cell, I stand alongside Stanley outside the Registry Office in the centre of Sheffield, he a dashing figure in smart new navy-blue suit, white shirt, black tie and gleaming brogues, a huge white carnation signifying the solemn occasion. Myself a demure bride in beige dress, matching coat and shoes, a pink carnation pinned against my lapel.

A new road ahead, signatures seal the bizarre relationship and, confetti dispersing on a gentle breeze, snapping cameras capture the occasion. Attended by a few close family members and a small group of Stanley's friends, the reception in the front room of Stanley's home on Foxhill is a quiet affair. However, the buzz of excitement, endless whirl of arrangements and anticipation finally triggers the switch, changing my personality, and against a background of popping corks, a sudden disturbance prompts a deathly hush. Champagne glass raised I journey into the past. Oblivious to shocked onlookers, I gaze at an imaginary scene outside the window, launching into a garbled account of the war and giggling manically throughout a one-sided conversation. Suddenly terrified by what I see, I thrust a trembling arm across my eyes, dipping my head low in a seeming attempt to escape an approaching missile. During that single, dramatic, moment many fears are realised. Some guests are frightened at the strange sight of me taking a trip back to an earlier time, others bemused, but the faulty mechanism swiftly correcting itself, my visit is fleeting and, turning away from the window, I smile, champagne glass raised in a toast to stunned onlookers. Ironically, as everyone else flounders, I am the only one in control and, totally oblivious to the brief aberration stunning others, I gently sip champagne, only the ticking of the clock breaking the uncomfortable silence.

A trembling hand firmly clamped across his mouth, Stanley gapes in stunned disbelief at my innocent composure! Having diced with the unknown, he frantically searches the room for much-needed support but, tactfully averting their gaze, some fumble for handkerchiefs nervously blowing their noses in their unease. Urgently checking the time, others make weak excuses and a hurried exit, and it's obvious they share his fears. Hurrying towards Stanley, his daughter, Sylvia, captures him in a firm embrace, tears streaming but a shrieking figure in beige, I lurch between them, screaming incoherently, of his infidelity. While two desperate people try to reason and calm my hysteria, Steven runs with his cry for help to the asylum, but its doors have finally been closed. Readily understanding the consequences of his impulsive act Stanley, immediately knows he has ensnared himself in a trap from which there is no escape and, sadly, what had begun as a day of celebration has ended with the terrible realisation that he has made a dreadful mistake.

Mentally damaged I am a millstone round his neck from the start. His life in turmoil, mine a minefield, we stumble through the days and, with no firm and constant guidance, I flounder when he is at work. Amidst mounting chaos, I find respite from confusion in endless cigarettes, severe warnings only temporarily curbing my carelessness and, my domestic skills frozen in time, even the most basic task poses a risk without supervision. Modern equipment making life easier for most, only complicate things for me. Electric washing machine, gas cooker and other gadgets, confusing and frightening, life is a struggle when left to my own devices, and Stanley worries about events at home throughout his working day.

Mind befuddled by medication, concentration limited, I carelessly leave lights burning all around the house and ears forever glued to the wireless, bills mount. Gas rings turned on, but left unlit, pose the risk of explosion with every match struck to light a cigarette, empty saucepans left on lit gas rings fill the house with acrid smoke and, flitting from task to task, I complete none. Every day is fraught with danger. Once kind, generous and tolerant, Stanley's nerves begin to fray and, forced to witness the gradual destruction of his previously immaculate home, he finally resumes full responsibility, banishing me to the tiny confines of the kitchen.

Cigarettes helping me wile away the days, once sweet-smelling rooms soon reeked with the putrid stench of stale tobacco, white walls turned a dingy shade of brown and original attraction fast fading, Stanley faces an intolerable future. Sometimes driven to complete distraction he turns me outdoors to walk the streets in all weathers but it's a frightening experience finding my way round unfamiliar surroundings.

Wiling away the hours, I stand peering through shop windows on Foxhill Road, gradually making my way to the open countryside to settle on a form overlooking Back Edge at Grenoside. Cigarette stubs gathering at my feet, I lazily gaze over surrounding fields and meadows and beyond the meandering River Don in the valley bottom towards the adjacent hillside climbing towards the far horizon. Distracted by childish laughter, I watch a young family pass behind me animatedly chattering on their way down the steep, winding slope of Jawbone Hill on their way to Oughtibridge Park. A cyclist negotiates a tricky bend before careering down the almost perpendicular slope, and passengers peering from the windows of a passing car, I feel incredibly lonely. Shades of night falling, the sun sinks to rest and, through fading light, I catch sight of a far distant clock tower rearing its head above surrounding trees. The asylum! The haunting scene momentarily sparks painful recall, immediately reminding of two decades of captivity and terrible suffering, but it's gone in a flash and, instantly turning away, I hurry back around the narrow bend of Jawbone Hill making my solitary way home.

No sight or sound of other human beings, only the occasional whinny of a horse hidden from view behind a high boundary hedge, hoot of a night owl startling me in the darkness, I wind my way around narrow country lanes making my way back to Foxhill and a night alone in the tiny back bedroom on Browning Road. Nerves in shreds and bitterly regretting his impetuosity, Stanley looks drawn with anguish at the prospect of a long, dark future and, growing ever more resentful at the shadow I cast over his life, his health begins to fail.

Weakened and burdened with dread he slips into a deep depression and a shadow of the former handsome, fit man, he succumbs to cancer. Terminal, it takes his life at speed and, forced to intervene, Social Services find me yet another home.

CHAPTER FOURTEEN
AT THE END – THE BEGINNING

Once the home of a wealthy Sheffield industrialist, Broomcroft has been converted for the care of the elderly, infirm and confused. An imposing stone building standing at the head of a winding driveway, huge bay windows overlook a mass of hydrangea and rhododendron bushes: rich red, crimson and blue flowers in full bloom. Tall oak, ash and larch filter sun through thick foliage, casting long, dark shadows over rolling lawns sloping towards Ecclesall Road way below. Bees, wasps and butterflies hover over colourful borders, birds sing, squirrels scamper up the trunks of trees and, in the shade of spreading branches, I drink in the heady wine of freedom.

Situated in the south of Sheffield, Broomcroft is far removed from everything familiar in the north but it has numerous advantages in its cloistered environment; its grandeur and warmth, a stark contrast to the chilling atmosphere of the asylum: welcoming atmosphere lifting me up to where I feel I more belong. Just inside the large entrance hall, a grand, winding stairway coils upward, coats hang on a carved stand in an alcove by the window and, though no fire burns in the grate of an ornate marble fireplace, it gives the impression of a real family living there. Sheet music rests on the stand of a highly polished walnut piano, strategically positioned so that light falls on the notes and vague memories momentarily stirred, I feel a strange desire to run my fingers across the keys but, no music in my soul, the moment quickly slips away.

Drawing in people from all walks of life, Broomcroft is a melting pot and, although thrust amongst others whose lives have been lived in stark contrast to my own, I fit in because there is no obvious distinction. Already in their dotage, some are also occasionally confused and, minds wandering, tolerate me in my momentary ramblings. From highly educated or wealthy backgrounds, some, whose families have long flown the nest and settled in far-flung places, have been left alone in fading years and, physically unable to cope, have made this place their home. Faculties intact, they keep in touch with world events through newspapers, radio or television and, indulging in intelligent conversation in my more lucid moments, I discover a part of me stifled for decades. Protected and without pressure I find tranquillity at last. Having tasted many of the worst flavours of life, I have learned humility and compassion, becoming a willing aide to the frail and elderly and listening to their woes and frustrations, draw on my own experience in order to understand and empathise. The right hand of those who struggle, I fetch and carry for the chair-bound, weak and confused, gaining a sense of fulfilment from usefulness. Content at last, peace of mind keeps the gremlins at bay and, winding my way up the grand stairway at night, I stand awhile at its final turn, peering through a beautiful stained-glass window into the darkness beyond. Cut in wonderful hues it lets in the light of numerous twinkling stars and, a brilliant yellow moon long providing the only constancy in my life, and nearing my harrowing journey's end, I finally face the night unafraid, morning with a warm glow inspired by the knowledge that I have, at last, found a role in life.

A happy spell at Broomcroft, cut short by sudden closure, my contentment is short-lived and, subsequently shunted from one Elderly Person's Home to another, I sit and wile away the hours amongst the often confused and elderly. Mere shelters, there are no beautiful grounds in which to walk, only pointless hours to kill and, caught in the destructive grip of boredom reminiscent of the past, my interest in life begins to fade. In failing health, I simply bide my time, grateful that the end of a traumatic, tortuous road is finally in sight.

Regular visitors over the years, my daughters prove a comfort in my fading days and, despite no bond from birth and long years of separation, my youngest looks down at me from a chair at the side of the bed. Smiling warmly, she leans forward and, reaching up, I gently draw her close and we both shed tears because life has robbed us both.

In these fading moments I ponder on the purpose of this seemingly pointless journey. Yet, is it pointless? Perhaps it's a time for reflection, for helping us come to terms with the trials and tribulations of a life already lived, in order to leave the world with peaceful mind. Yet how can I come to terms with the fact that, left alone in the world, I became a helpless victim of medical science? A guinea pig for cruel experiments on the human brain, permanently stripping me of every semblance of normality and, worst of all, the chance to regain it. My powers of reasoning strangely returned in my final moments, however, I can now see clearly how those wild, inane ramblings during my times of utter helplessness in my fight to save my family, crazy battles against admittance to the asylum and wild, frantic behaviour when strapped in a straitjacket or thrust into a padded cell could be interpreted as madness, but they were the desperate acts of a woman trapped and totally out of control of her life.

Somewhere deep in the vaults of the asylum will be recorded a story of a sad, pathetic mad woman and some will remember me being hauled from home in a straitjacket and bundled into a tell-tale Black Maria or, as that peculiar individual strutting strangely around the streets of Sheffield after that fatal cut, but behind it all is a story, and maybe one day it may be told. Indeed, having lived amongst inmates for decades, I wonder how many more stories lie behind those sad and desperate people incarcerated in lunatic asylums, many possibly fighting the same desperate battle for freedom in their helplessness and subsequently plied with medication and shock treatment to subdue them until rendered infantile and easier to control. Will we ever know?

Unexpectedly, this final gift of hindsight has proved invaluable in my dying moments because in full knowledge of the fact that there are no means of changing what has gone, I have gained acceptance. In fact, though harrowing, this journey has proved strangely cathartic laying the ghosts of the past and, curtains beginning to close on the final scene, I at last feel life's heavy burden being carried away on a huge sigh as the bright light gradually fades into blackness. A warm blanket of complete peace enveloping me, I willingly let go of my long, miserable life.

Dear Reader

If you enjoyed reading this it would be great if you could do a quick review on Amazon, Goodreads or whatever book review sites you use: a line or two would be great. Reviews and personal recommendations are really appreciated by authors and small publishers and help us to keep doing what we do. Thanks.

Milton Keynes UK
Ingram Content Group UK Ltd.
UKHW041006140923
428666UK00001B/10